THE WILD, WILD WEST OF
LOUIS L'AMOUR

The Illustrated Guide to Cowboys, Indians, Gunslingers, Outlaws and Texas Rangers

BRUCE WEXLER

AN IMPRINT OF RUNNING PRESS
PHILADELPHIA • LONDON

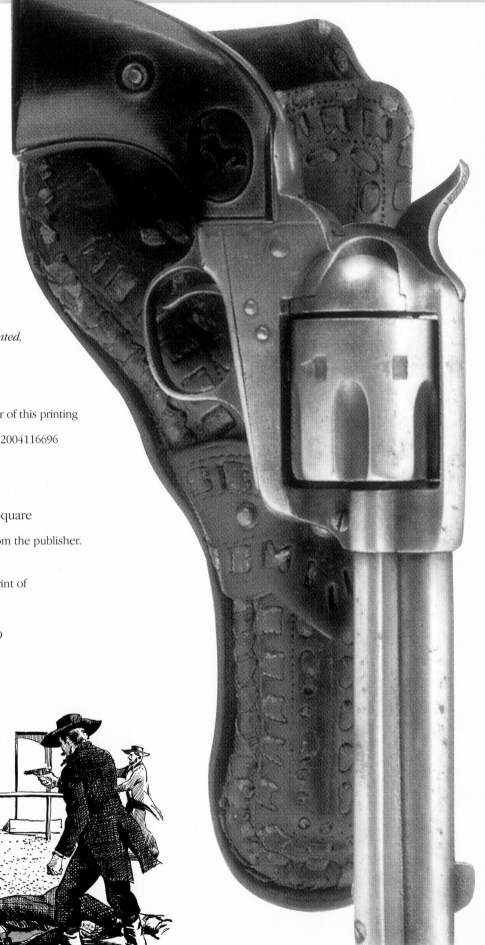

9 8 7 6 5 4 3 2 1
Digit on the right indicates the number of this printing

Library of Congress Control Number: 2004116696

ISBN 0-7624-2357-9

Designed by Philip Clucas MSIAD

Color Reproduction by Berkeley Square

This book may be ordered by mail from the publisher.
But try your bookstore first!

Published by Courage Books, an imprint of
Running Press Book Publishers
125 South Twenty-second Street
Philadelphia, Pennsylvania 19103-4399

Visit us on the web!
www.runningpress.com

Contents

The Laureate of the Lariat
A biography of Louis L'Amour

Above: Louis L'Amour in later life. Still a cowboy.

Louis L'Amour, the man destined to become an American national treasure in his own lifetime, was born on March 22, 1908, just as the final days of the American frontier were playing themselves out. Louis Dearborn LaMoore was the youngest of seven children born to Dr. Louis Charles LaMoore and Emily Dearborn LaMoore in Jamestown, North Dakota. His family were of French-Irish stock, and he claimed himself as a descendant of Francois Rene, Vicompte de Chateaubriand, writer, statesman, and well-known epicure.

Jamestown was a substantial farming community, and Louis's father was a large animal vetinariary surgeon. He had come to the territory in 1882. He later went on

> ### 'Louis L'Amour was the kind heart of America. The walking, talking, smiling and story-telling best of what we like to think we really are.'
> #### HARLAN ELLISON

to sell farm machinery and manage harvesting crews. But Jamestown was also a hub on the Northern Pacific Railroad and the LaMoore brothers often encountered cowboys on their way back West, travelling to their ranches in western North Dakota, or on their way East to cattle markets with full stockcars. Dr. LaMoore became very involved in this traffic as a state Livestock Inspector, certifying the health of the cattle in transit.

But Louis's closest contact with the Old West and his frontiersman heritage was through his maternal grandfather, Abraham Truman Dearborn, who lived in a little house at the back of the LaMoore property. He had fought in both the Civil and Indian Wars, and two of his sons had worked on cattle ranches. Besides this, Abraham was also in contact with many Indians who came to visit, drinking copious cups of tea and coffee with him. This is rather ironic, in view of the fact that Louis's great grandfather met his end by being scalped by a Sioux Indian in North Dakota. Louis later credited his grandfather and his old-timer friends with bringing him up in an atmosphere rich with tales and stories of life on the American Frontier. After his grandfather died, the Indians melted away.

Education was highly valued in the LaMoore household (Louis's mother had been trained as a teacher), and the entire family was intelligent and well read. Emily was well known locally as an avid reader, storyteller, and amateur poet. The infant

Louis was taught to read by his beloved sister Emmy Lou, who died young in the Spanish flu epidemic of 1918. The family culture certainly rubbed off onto the embryonic storyteller. Dr. LaMoore loved horses and dogs, and taught his youngest son the ways of the animal kingdom. He was also a personal inspiration to his son, instilling him with a deep belief in hard work and self- reliance. Dr. LaMoore also taught all of his sons to box, something that both shaped Louis's early life, and turns up in several of his characters, while he was also a spiritual man that taught Sunday school. Louis's siblings also exerted their influence on the youngest member of the family. His elder brother Parker was a newspaperman, and a reportage-like edge certainly found its way into Louis's writing, as did several honorable members of the press. As for Louis's other siblings, his brother Yale managed a grocery store, where Louis and his adopted brother John often earned a little pocket money. Twin sisters Clara and Clarice had died in infancy, while elder sister Edna worked as a librarian at the Alfred Dickey Free Library, later moving away from the family home to pursue a career as a schoolteacher.

This supportive and dynamic family encouraged the young Louis to become a voracious reader and enabled him to become a largely self-educated man. He supplemented the three hundred book home library (that contained works by Whittier, Lowell, Longfellow, Poe, and the five-volume 'Collier's History of the World') with copious volumes from the Alfred Dickey Free Library, and read extremely widely. Louis was mostly attracted by books on history and the natural sciences, the informative Little Blue Books of E. Haldeman-Julius, but was also captivated by the fictional works of Robert Louis Stevenson, Jack London, Charles Dickens, and Edgar Rice Burroughs. These were books just like his own later works, filled with tales of adventure, hardship,

and epic survival, but also infused with humanity and deep emotion. By the end of his life, L'Amour was to have a collection of more than 10,000 volumes, mostly books on history and archaeology, to which he referred constantly in the course of his writing. Louis expressed his all-consuming belief in the importance of books passionately: 'Books are the building blocks of civilization, for without the written word, a man knows nothing beyond what occurs during his own brief years and, perhaps, in a few tales his parents tell him.'

But the subliminal effect of his family background was just as fundamental to Louis, instilling deep and irrevocable feelings of family loyalty, duty, and a clear sense of right and wrong. These are not only characteristics that clung to the man himself throughout his life, but shine through in many of his heroes, who are often either deeply aware of their own roots, or else yearning for a family to belong to. He also grew to epitomize the adage that education is the key to success and a good life – though he was also living proof that this didn't necessarily need to be of the formal academic kind, having more the 'Education of a Wandering Man.'

But, as for so many American families, things got really tough for the LaMoore family in the 1920s, and they moved on to Oklahoma, looking for better prospects. It was at this point that the fifteen-year-old Louis decided to leave home, not wishing to be a burden on his parents. He also decided to revert to the original family name of L'Amour, which his father had anglicized. For a man who grew up to be a professional writer, honored by President Reagan with a Congressional Gold Medal and the Presidential Medal of Freedom, and to be awarded an honorary doctorate

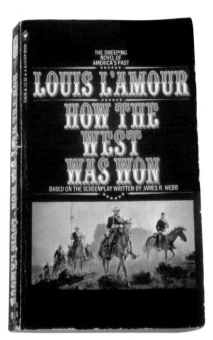

Above: An edition of HOW THE WEST WAS WON from the early '70s, the author's own well-thumbed copy.

in literature by Jamestown College, he hadn't even made it through to the end of tenth grade. His education now became less formal, but more character forming. His stated main aim was to 'see the country,' and he set off on a twenty-year adventure that was to become a fund of stories that he would develop into his published work. As he said, 'My stories have come from incidents in my own life, anecdotes I've heard, stories repeated by miners, cowhands, Indians, and others whom I've known.'

Essentially, during this period, he lived the life of one of his own Louis L'Amour heroes. A big powerful man, already over six-foot tall in his teens, he took any number of back breaking and dangerous jobs. Longshoreman, ranch hand, lumberjack, circus elephant handler, fruit picker, hay shocker, flume builder, railroad worker (for the Southern Pacific Railroad), and gold prospector. He hopped freight trains with men who had been riding the tracks for over half a century, packing his clothes with newspaper to keep warm. L'Amour also travelled from town to town fighting professionally as a bare-knuckle boxer. He won all but five of his fifty-nine professional bouts, forty-five of them with knockouts, claiming that he 'never lost a fight when I was eating regularly.' He won the biggest purse of his career, $1,800, in Singapore, winning by a knockout after seven rounds. He later characterized these times as 'rough years; often I was hungry, out of work and facing situations such as I have written about.' In writing his autobiography, his son Beau describes how he searched out the 'homes, hotel rooms, boarding houses, auto courts, lumber piles, and hobo jungles where Louis slept as a youth.' But as well as a wealth of experience from which he could draw, these chequered experiences were also the crucible in which the man, Louis L'Amour,

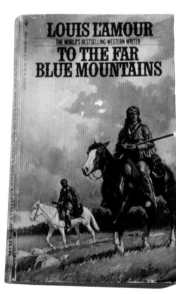

Below: The author's copy of TO THE FAR BLUE MOUNTAINS. An edition from the '70s.

was formed. The same man that illuminates his books; warm, modest, and straight.

He travelled extensively during this time: biking across India along the route followed by Rudyard Kipling's character, Kim, travelling throughout Europe, sailing around the Far East as a merchant seaman; circumnavigating the world on a freighter, sailing a dhow on the Red Sea, visiting Egypt, being shipwrecked in the West Indies, and being stranded for twenty-two desperate days in the blazing Mojave Desert. All kinds of stories emanate from this colorful period of his life, including a well-circulated tale that he used the proceeds of a Macao-an treasure trove to fund a trip to Paris and the great cultural cities of Europe.

But he also often returned home to America and travelled all over the dirt roads of the West working as a miner, lumberjack, and ranch hand, saying 'I was all over the West that way.' He described the most difficult time of this period of his life as the three months when he was on shore in San Pedro, between ships, and completely broke. He was forced to sleep in boxcars and under piles of lumber and to go without eating for days at a time. Stories from these days turned up later in his book YONDERING – 'I didn't beg or steal, just went without… I have a penchant for stories about survival, lessons in survival. I've been a survivor for most of my life.'

These years of peripatetic freedom gave depth and complexity to both the man and his writing, together with a feeling of conflict often manifested by many L'Amour heroes when it comes time to settle down. Linus Rawlings epitomizes this in HOW THE WEST WAS WON. Even though deep love draws him into domestic life, he can't forget the call of the woods and wild places.

In the late 1930s and now approaching his thirties, Louis finally returned to the family home in Choctaw, Oklahoma, deciding to follow the family tradition of settling down to become a writer. Louis reckoned that he had 'wanted to write from the time I could walk' and claimed that since 1816, thirty-three members of his family had been writers of one kind or another. His family background and personal experience of wanderlust all seemed to culminate in his desire to write stories. Louis had sold his first short story 'Anything for a Pal' in 1935, and sold several other articles during his wandering years, including the 1937 story 'Gloves for a Tiger' to *Thrilling Adventures Magazine*, and 'The Admiral' to *Story*. He gradually became a regular contributor to Western 'pulp' magazines, using the name 'Jim Mayo.'

Publishing short stories in magazines was a direct response to the difficult economic conditions of the time. There was a huge demand for this kind of escapist literature in the '30s, and a huge range of magazines was offered for sale. Louis deliberately chose to submit his work to the popular 'pulps' because highbrow literary magazines didn't pay their contributors at all, and although the middle market 'slicks' (magazines printed on shiny coated paper) paid better rates, they only remitted the money to the author on publication, and often required extensive rewrites.

On the other hand, the rates paid by the 'pulps' (named for their rough, 'pulp' paper) were lower, but they paid their contributors promptly (within fourteen days of submission) and usually required the author to prepare a single draft. To a man like Louis L'Amour, living on the bread line, this prompt payment and quick turnaround was critical.

The volume of stories required by this market also meant that writers had to come up with a large number of ideas quickly, an inventive skill that Louis was to retain throughout his career. Several of L'Amour's 'pulp' short stories were later extended into complete novels. Beau L'Amour recounts how the short story 'The Gift of the Cochise' was later developed into HONDO, Louis L'Amour's first really

successful Western novel. HONDO was published in 1953 and was made into a film starring John Wayne, who described the book as the 'Best western novel I have read.' By 1983, the book had sold 2,300,000 copies.

Beau also describes how his father occasionally risked his working time and money, writing stories specifically for the 'slicks,' balancing the cost of the postage against the better rates paid by these classier publications. But he generally found that writing in the tried and tested action formulae required by the pulps was far less risky.

But back in 1939, Louis's first officially published book, SMOKE FROM THIS ALTAR, was something completely different, a book of poems inspired by his global tour. But despite its rather surprising format, the book can most accurately be described as 'vintage L'Amour storytelling – in verse – about nature, the land, and the people who loved and braved it.' The book was originally available only in Oklahoma bookstores. Although not a commercial success, it attracted good reviews, and he was commended for his 'love for words, industry and something to say' by the *Daily Oklahoma* reviewer.

Louis L'Amour was a practitioner of 'The kind of storytelling that makes the wolves come out of the woods to listen.' PEOPLE MAGAZINE

But after just a couple of years, L'Amour's nascent writing career was interrupted by the outbreak of WWII. He joined the army in 1942 and following two years stationed in the States, served overseas as (amongst other things) a Lieutenant in the 3622 Quartermaster Truck Company, posted as part of a tank destroyer unit on front line positions in France and Germany. These were also formative experiences for Louis that turned up in YONDERING.

Like so many men of his generation, L'Amour had to start his life again on his return from active duty. In 1946, he settled in Los Angeles, now almost forty. He immediately began to submit detective stories, tales of adventure, Western yarns, and sports anecdotes to various magazines in the hope of publication. Short stories formed the backbone of his work in the years 1946-50, but this genre gradually fell victim to the upsurge in TV ownership and pressure from radio drama and paperback books, so Louis was obliged to change his metier. He first graduated to novel writing by producing four Hopalong Cassidy novels using the pseudonym Tex Burns. These books were based on the 'Hopalong' character that had originally been created by Clarence Mulford (who wrote 28 'Hopalong' books between 1907 and 1941). Louis refused to acknowledge these books for several years, because the original idea had not been his own. But this slightly embarrassing episode was crucial in pointing the way to Louis's true genre – that of the Western novel, and indeed the four 'Hopalong' titles were re-published in the early 1990s and remain available.

This 'westerly' creative direction was reinforced by the advice of an editor L'Amour met a New York cocktail party, who advised Louis to concentrate on

'My books are for the people who do the work of the world, who struggle to make ends meet, who build, the people who do!' LOUIS L'AMOUR

writing down the frontier tales with which he had enthralled him. Initially, L'Amour had his reservations about pursuing this style of writing – he knew that the critics never took Western literature seriously, but ultimately decided to 'take the ball and run with it' and make sure that his books

became the best of their kind, and bestsellers. 'No one ever went into writing with a more calculated career attitude than I did' he said, recalling how he determined to keep his name in front of the public by keeping a constant stream of new novels on offer. Fortuitously, the '50s were the heyday of the paperback Western, and Louis determined to be the next great exponent of the genre.

L'Amour's first Western novel, WESTWARD THE TIDE was published in England in 1950. But his real breakthrough came when he encountered Saul David, the editorial director of Bantam Books. David recalls how they met for the first time in the Beverly Hills Hotel, Louis bringing a selection of writing from HONDO to show him. David says the material 'knocked me out. I signed him to a long-term contract on the spot.' HONDO was published in 1953. According to David, the only problem was Louis's name, his superiors in New York thought L'Amour much too fluffy for a hard Western writer, like a 'Western written in lipstick'- and his next two books SHOWDOWN AT YELLOW BUTTE (1953) and UTAH BLAINE (1954) were published under the pseudonym of Jim Mayo. But this was soon abandoned in favor of 'Louis L'Amour,' and no soft editor from New York was unwise enough to mention 'lipstick' to the bare-knuckle prize- fighter from North Dakota.

From the start, Louis was acutely aware that novel writing is an extremely competitive field, with authors fighting for the attention of the public. Plus, book publishing itself has to struggle for a share of the entertainment market. To this end, he made a conscious decision that he would grab the reader from the very first sentence of every book, and ensure that his stories were 'unputdownable' right to the end. A key element to this was complete transparency of style. 'If you can read something and it's so simple and clear that you think you could write it better, you can bet you can't.'

This consciousness of the audience meant that from his first book, Louis aimed to forge a deep bond with his reader, by telling his stories simply, in a staccato style bereft of long internal monologues and descriptive passages, relying instead on pace and plot to enthral. He also deliberately refrained from offending with gratuitous sex, profanity, and violence. Just as Louis had anticipated, his style was dismissed by the literary establishment of the time. But L'Amour had effectively circumvented critical acclaim to make a solemn contract with his readership, which was by far and away the most important thing to him as a writer.

This mutual loyalty persists to this day. All of his 101 books remain in print, over thirty of his novels have been made into movies (between 1953 and 1971), and an estimated 225 million copies of his titles are in print. From the beginning, his creative pace never abated. From the publication of his first novel, L'Amour averaged three or four books a year, and never retired, dying during the composition of BORDEN CHANTRY II (the sequel to his classic earlier novel). Several L'Amour novels and other works, including THE SACKETT COMPANION were published posthumously, and collections of his works are compiled and released to this day.

Louis's son Beau very interestingly describes his father's day-to-day creative process. Louis would begin a novel with just a scene, or the beginning of a story, genuinely not knowing where this would take him. If the first chapter kept his interest as he knocked it out, he assumed that the reader would feel the same, and he kept going with it. If not, he would discard the idea to a slush pile, and turn his attention to another project. Fragments of stories rattled around for literally decades before he got around to writing these fully. Beau also describes how, upon Louis's death, he came upon hundreds of incomplete stories, fragments of discarded plots and themes that had never been developed. This is a real reflection of just how prolific Louis L'Amour was throughout his long career. He was at his typewriter by seven every day of his life including weekends and holidays, writing five to ten pages each day. Nor was he precious about his writing environment, claiming that he 'could sit in the middle of Sunset Boulevard and write with my typewriter on my knees; temperamental I am not.' To some extent, his ferocious work rate was necessitated by financial imperatives. It wasn't until the '70s that L'Amour was earning what Beau describes as a 'good living,' although, by this time, he had published some of his most popular and archetypal novels. These included a good part of the fantastically successful Sackett saga and the seminal works SHALAKO, CATLOW, CHANCY, and THE EMPTY LAND. It wasn't until 1973 that the family were able to move house to a more up-market Los Angeles neighbor- hood, by which time Louis was 65. He finally felt independent and financially secure for the first time in his life, and in the literary market place, he was outselling even popular authors like James Michener. Around this time, Louis signed a thirty- book contract with Bantam to keep himself in employment, and working to a series of deadlines.

L'Amour himself believed that the crux of his popularity was his extreme attention to authenticity. 'The West was wilder than any man can write it, but my facts, my terrain, my guns, my Indians are real. I've ridden and hunted the country. When I write about a spring, that spring is there, and the water is good to drink.' He always researched every book, wherever it was set, and the Western novels were often based in the minutiae of contemporary diaries and newspapers and the stories of 'old timers' for absolute veracity. 'His readers felt that he had walked the land the characters did' said Stuart Applebaum, Louis's Bantam editor at the time of his death. But it wasn't only the terrain that

Louis L'Amour is 'the only movable piece of Mount Rushmore.'
SAUL DAVID

'Writing is sharing. I'm working for the reader.'
LOUIS L'AMOUR

Louis wanted to bring to life as accurately as possible. He actively sought out old gunfighters and outlaws, eventually knowing thirty or thirty-five of them personally, and interviewed every kind of

'Louis L'Amour has become part of our cultural consciousness.'

DONALD DALE JACKSON

frontier character. It was his proud claim that 'I am probably the last writer who will ever have known the people who lived the frontier life…They'd be standoffish at first, but I'd keep talking and they'd warm up and tell me wonderful stories. I heard that when Zane Grey travelled the West he always 'made his own campfire,' and kept his distance. I wasn't like that. I was one of them.' Saul David accurately described his style as though he was writing for 'people just beyond the campfire of his typewriter.'

In his trawl for authentic Western characters, Louis met five people who had met Billy The Kid, including the woman who prepared his body for the grave. He also talked with Emmett Dalton of the Dalton Gang, Tom Pickett (whose claim to fame was that he had had his thumb shot off in the Lincoln County War), Elgagio Baca, a New Mexican lawyer who had fought a famous gunfight with over eighty of Tom Slaughter's cowboys, and Jeff Milton of the Arizona Border Patrol who had been a Texas Ranger, together with Jim Roberts the last survivor of the Tonto Basin War, who later became the Marshal of Jerome, Arizona. He also developed a huge regard for the original cowboys, believing that they were far from the illiterate men on horseback of popular folklore, but rather men who were drawn West (from Europe or the Eastern US) by a romantic ideal, only to experience a brutally hard life of grindingly hard work.

Personally, L'Amour's life revolved around the same loadstars as those of his heroes – home and family. He waited until

'Our professor emeritus of how the West was won.'

MORLEY SAFER

he had a little more financial stability before marrying his wife, aspiring actress Katherine Elizabeth Adams in 1956, who had appeared in several plays and TV's 'Gunsmoke' and 'Death Valley Days.' Kathy was the daughter of a resort developer and silent movie star and had grown up roving the deserts and mountains of Southern California. They set up home in a relatively modest house in Los Angeles, on the proceeds from the successful Sackett series. Kathy willingly gave up her own career to travel with Louis and serve as his personal assistant, and he gave her a good deal of credit for helping him with his the research by which he held such store. She said 'I feel that the most rewarding, the most adventurous, the most exciting, the most fun thing I ever did was to marry Louis.' Theirs was a lifelong partnership. Kathy acted as her husband's literary agent for the final thirty years of his life, and became President of Louis L'Amour Enterprises after his death. The couple had two children, Beau Dearborn (in 1961) and Angelique Gabrielle (in 1964).

By 1981, Louis was one of the five best-selling authors still working, in a select coterie including Harold Robbins, Barbara Cartland, Irving Wallace, and Janet Dailey, outselling any other Western writer. He is now reckoned to be the third top-selling author in the world, translated into dozens of languages. He never stopped developing his craft, believing that he was only achieving 'full command' of his powers as he reached his seventies. Even then, he was described as being 'still ruggedly handsome… with eyebrows that peak in gray-brown arrowheads. He wears Western shirts and string ties and cowboy boots and speaks in a measured, confident baritone.' Although Louis ultimately had all the trappings of success, and received massive adulation from his huge fan base, he never received critical acclaim in his lifetime. Just like Dickens and Shakespeare, his work was dismissed as lowbrow, and the fact that, like them, he wrote with a financial imperative snapping at his heels until relatively late in his writing career, seemed to result in his work not being taken seriously in a critical sense. In many ways, Dickens and L'Amour have a great deal in common. Both wrote episodically for the 'pulps' of their day and were hard working professionals, with no hint of dilettantism. Both were hounded by the need to earn a living for their families, and took this responsibility very seriously. Their own lives were very much reflected in what they wrote, and their fictional heroes often seem to achieve resolution to difficulties experienced in their own lives.

Despite the admiration of several Presidents, including Dwight D. Eisenhower, Johnson, Gerald Ford, Jimmy Carter, and Ronald Reagan, this lack of critical respect seems to have been the source of some irritation to Louis. He was determined that his work was indeed 'literature,' and said 'I don't give a damn what anyone else thinks,' he said 'I know it's literature and it know it will be read 100 years from now.'

Although he lived and worked in Los Angeles until the end of his life, Louis's later financial success enabled him to buy a tract of land in the West of his imagination. He purchased Maggie Rock in 1983, together with the surrounding 1,800 acres.

Although THE WILD, WILD WEST OF LOUIS L'AMOUR concentrates on the themes and ideas developed in his Western novels, which form the hub of his output, several of his later works inhabited different worlds altogether. Medieval Europe is the backdrop for THE WALKING DRUM (1984), the supernatural thriller HAUNTED MESA (1988) is set in the contemporary Southwest, and the LAST OF THE BREED (1986) evokes the Siberian landscape of Lake Baikal. But L'Amour's attention to detail and authenticity remains a paramount consideration throughout his work. 'If my book is set in 1600, I write so that someone who lived then would

recognize the road I'm describing.' This is literally true. The sixteenth-century London evoked in TO THE FAR BLUE MOUNTAINS (1977) is completely historically accurate – the Prospect of Whitby pub was there then, and you can take a drink in this Thames-side hostelry to this very day.

Louis died in June 1988, tragically falling victim to lung cancer, though a lifelong non-smoker. His doctors attributed the disease to harmful dust to which he had been exposed during his time as a miner. He continued to write throughout his illness, starting work on EDUCATION OF A WANDERING MAN only after being diagnosed as terminally ill. The only concession he made to his failing health was to move work from his office to a desk in an upstairs bedroom, and finally into the master bedroom. He was editing WANDERING MAN only hours before he died, a few days after being told that his sales had topped the two hundred million mark, outselling John Steinbeck 5:1. His death has done nothing to stem his popularity. 'Louis L'Amour' is now an international brand, with its own credit card and merchandising empire.

Louis enjoyed eighty years of a 'one-of-a-kind life lived to the fullest,' and his life 'inspired the books that will forever enable us to relive our glorious frontier heritage.' Latterly, he had also enjoyed fame, fortune, and recognition of his extraordinary creative stature. But, like one of his own heroes, L'Amour had retained a modest demeanor, shunning the Tinsel Town lifestyle in favor of the clean stillness of the mountains.

By the end of his life, Louis L'Amour the man and Louis L'Amour the author were almost completely interchangeable. His daughter, Angelique, said that 'By reading his words, each reader has met a part of my father. Each hero has a bit of Dad's experience that makes him who he is.'

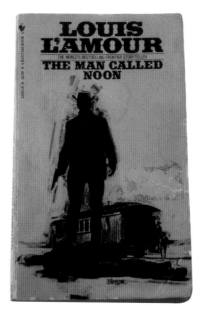

Above: The author's copy of THE MAN CALLED NOON, with a typical cover from the early '80s.

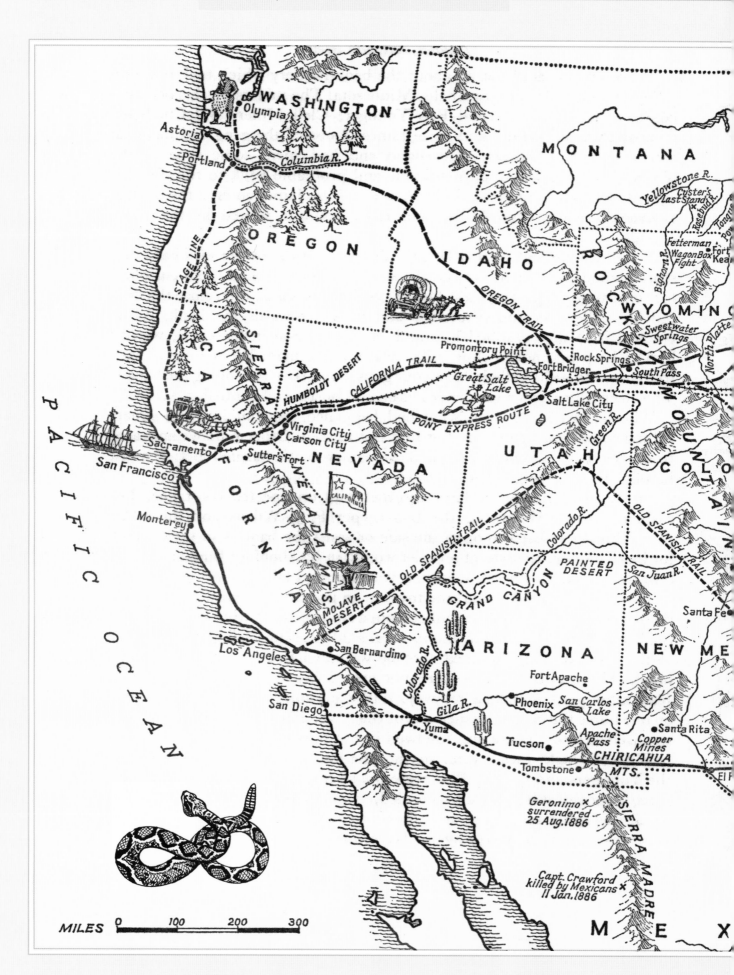

The Way West

The American West 'is a dream. It is what people who have come here from the beginning of time have dreamed... it is a landscape that has to be seen to be believed, and may have to be believed to be seen.'

KIOWA POET N. SCOTT MOMADAY

Above: The hanging of a pirate at Wapping Dock in London. Black Tom Watkins flees England to avoid this fate.

Right: The pure grandeur and beauty of America awaiting those brave enough to make the ocean crossing.

Perhaps the single most important theme that drives Louis L'Amour's Western novels is the Way West itself.

The first settlers from the Old World voyaged West across the ocean to the shores of America. They were almost always in search of a free life in the New World, and were often hounded by injustice and undeserved troubles. There is a clear sense in L'Amour's work that their first landfall in the East also became corrupted, necessitating a move further West across the face of America itself. A journey once more driven by the need for freedom, land, and opportunity; intertwined with a certain indefinable longing for a pure and simple life.

Written over seventeen novels and ten generations, the Sackett family saga is a fantastic evocation of both of these strands of westward emigration. In TO THE FAR BLUE MOUNTAINS, Barney Sackett follows the example of the Pilgrim Fathers by risking everything to reach 'Raleigh's Land,' to escape a corrupt and oppressive regime. Barney has been imprisoned, and threatened with torture to force a confession to crimes he hasn't committed. He is accused of the murder of the influential but villainous Genester

(although this was actually the result of an honorable duel) and is also (wrongly) suspected of having stolen the lost royal treasure of the Wash. He is forced to realize that in a debased society, even a law-abiding man can't always look to the law of the land for protection. His travelling companion, Black Tom Watkins, faces the gallows for smuggling. This was a virtually universal 'crime' practiced by many wealthy people, churchmen and lawyers, but for which only the poor are punished. The upshot of this is, that for Tom and Barney, the 'forest' of the untamed new territory 'seems safer than the London streets' where injustice and persecution lurk in the shadows.

Sackett's followers have less pressing, but equally heart felt reasons for their journeys. As John Quill says, the wide open spaces of America promise 'So much land, and so few people, when in our country people long for the land and have none, for its all belongs to the great lords. Even the wild game is theirs.' The practice of 'enclosing' land had indeed led to the dispossession of the English peasantry. It had begun in the Middle Ages, and led to the virtual enslavement of the vast majority of the population.

Below: A fake bank note satirizing Britain's readiness to hang felons for even the smallest of crimes.

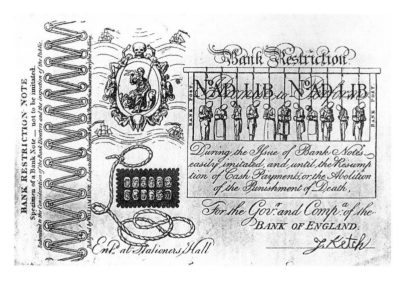

Men were obliged to labour unpaid for the local landowners, in very fields that had once been theirs. Poaching even wild animals for the pot was a capital crime, punishable by hanging.

Above: The rigors of the sea passage meant that new immigrants were ready to face almost anything.

Even by the late sixteenth century, when Barney decides to make his break for freedom, there were only very limited opportunities for personal improvement. People's destinies were almost entirely circumscribed by their birth and social position. Little wonder then that a resourceful, intelligent, and courageous man like Sackett yearns for the chance to lead a 'wild, free life,' unfettered by social convention.

Typically for a Louis L'Amour hero, the only element of 'civilization' that Barney considers important enough to carry to America is a selection of books, so that he will have 'a chance to listen to the words of other men who had lived their lives, to share with them trials and troubles.' These include the bible and his father's favorite, Plutarch. L'Amour strongly implies that men like Sackett who had 'some impulse… some selective device that chose (them)… to venture' effectively defined the character of the New World itself. For only men of his stamp, who were both intellectually and practically capable ('my hands are cunning with tools'), would be able to survive without the trappings of society. As Black Tom Watkins says, the 'entry into a new land is a hard, hard thing.' Strength of character is also a recurring theme in L'Amour's Western novels. Although the action of HANGING WOMAN CREEK takes place a couple of centuries later, Irishman Philo Farley restates L'Amour's belief in personal merit over background and social status, 'Over there (in England), education and position seem the most important things, but out here… well, it's the way it should be everywhere – character comes first… stamina, courage, and a strong sense of justice.' Sadly, for Philo, the immigrant experience leads only to death, although his sister marries into the Western way of life.

Prospective settlers first had to brave the hardship of the voyage itself. Barney Sackett tries to keep this in perspective by recounting even more epic voyages undertaken in earlier times: 'men had sailed farther, long before. The Malays had sailed from the islands south of the Equator, from Java and Sumatra to Madagascar. And Cheng Ho, the eunuch from the court of Imperial China, had sailed five times to Africa before Columbus or Vasco Da Gama.' He is also an explorer, following in their footsteps. Like them, he steps out of the known

world into only vaguely charted territory. The belief that the world was flat had only lately been abandoned, although Barney insists that this idea was not one that had had much credit with 'seafaring' men, 'It was a tale told to landsmen, or to merchants who might be inclined to compete for markets.'

But Barney seems unwilling to credit himself with an entirely conscious impetus to make for the new land. As he says, and this very much sounds like the conviction of L'Amour himself, 'Since the beginning of time men have moved across the face of the world, and we like to believe this is a result of our individual will, our choice, and it may be so, but might it not be that we are moved by tides buried in our natures? Tides we cannot resist?' It sounds entirely cogent that a man's subliminal nature may well be the driving force that sets out to shape the new continent. This is also typical of the modesty of the classic L'Amour hero. Generally, only fools and criminals are arrogant and over-confident in his books.

But despite his flight from the stifling restraint of the Old World, Barney does not wish to break with his own past, or that of his family. For although he believes

Above: A group of immigrants photographed while waiting to board ship at Plymouth harbor, England. The first phase of their journey West.

'pride of title or family is an empty thing,' he retains a value in family tradition, 'for a child without tradition is a child crippled before the world.' This so truly reflects America's immigrant tradition, where in-coming families have been forced to abandon everything but their customs and pride in their family origin.

Even having made it to the New World, the Sackett contingent continue their way West, overtaking those who have already settled on the Easter Seaboard. He still doesn't feel safe from his past. Though he finally makes it to the Blue Mountains, this is only to die by Indian attack. But nevertheless, Barney has left a signpost for his descendants to follow.

Like so many other Americans, the Sackett clan continue their westward journey over the centuries. L'Amour characterizes the pull of the 'fair, wild land' as being that of freedom and self-respect, away from corruption and injustice. The same hunger for a clean life, and self- determination (particularly symbolized by land ownership) impelled so many families, of all kinds of different backgrounds, to keep trekking. 'There's a new land yonder where there are no lords or gamekeepers, and the air had the flavor of freedom in it.'

These Pages: The immigrants to the 'fair, wild land' met with Native Americans from various tribes, who had been on the continent for thousands of years. Barney Sackett understands that the Indians can teach the new arrivals many things about the land.

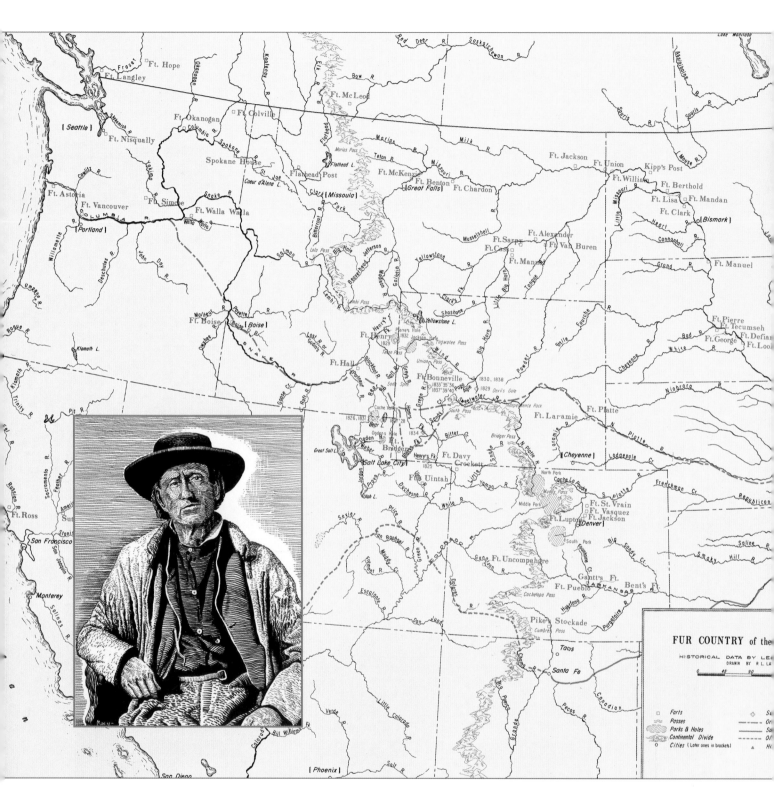

Above: A map of the Fur Country of the West, with an inset picture of Jim Bridger. Trappers helped to map the new territory.

In the very first Sackett novel published, THE DAYBREAKERS, brothers Tyrell and Orrin continue the family trek westward after the Civil War, escaping from the poverty and blood feuds of the Tennessee Mountains. Ultimately, they bring law and order to a swathe of the new territory.

The same hunger for freedom, land and opportunity that inspired the Sacketts infuses L'Amour's great tour de force HOW THE WEST WAS WON. By the nineteenth century, the East is almost as densely settled as Europe itself, and the rules of Society are almost as fixed and relentless. It's certainly no place for the

Rockies bought for $15 million from Napoleon. Jefferson was fascinated by everything from dinosaurs to fine wine, but had been spellbound by tales of the West from his boyhood, and had amassed the largest collection of books about the region on earth. He now persuaded Congress to authorize $2,500, to finance the westward expedition of adventurers Meriwether Lewis (Jefferson's personal secretary, a skilled hunter and amateur scientist) and William Clark (Jefferson's old army commander and talented woodsman) across this newly acquired land. Jefferson told them that the chief object of their mission was to find the (non-existent) Northwest Passage, but they ended up being the first Americans to cross the Rockies, finding the overland way to the West. Their courage blazed a trail for other men such as Kit Carson, Jim Bridger, Bill Williams, Joe Walker... and L'Amour's own heroes, of course.

Both Left: Meriwether Lewis and William Clark were charged with discovering the Northwest Passage, but became the first Americans to cross the Rockies.

Below: Kit Carson, another famous mountain man who helped open up the trails to the West.

rugged individualists that populate Louis L'Amour's imagination. But the historical tide of events turns in their favor.

L'Amour describes how the whole psychology of a nation was reinvigorated by President Thomas Jefferson's Louisiana Purchase of 1803: 800,000 square miles of territory between the Mississippi and the

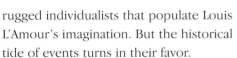

Opposite Page: Many Indian tribes were hugely helpful to the early western pioneers. Amongst other things, they taught them how to use canoes to get around the new land. Others were less well disposed to the white insurgents.

Above and right: A well-equipped frontiersman stands proud in the unspoiled and virgin territory.

These rugged, westward moving frontiersmen and women were cut from the very same cloth as L'Amour's own antecedents. He strongly maintained that 'there was no period in the world's history that is so fascinating as the era in which the American West was opening up.'

In HOW THE WEST WAS WON, there is a strong feeling that an entire continent is responding to some magnetic westward impulse. Hawkins, the Ohio River pirate, graphically describes the trek West as a

'colossal binge, a gigantic migration…
The world has never seen the like, folks
from all the lands of creation, streamin'
west, flowin' like a great tide, some of
them walkin', some drivin' wagons, and
some a-horseback… to populate a new
land.' But there is an undercurrent of
fear, for 'no new land is gained without
blood and suffering… how many would
die before the West was won?' The
Prescott family, around whom the
different sections of the book revolve,
board a boat in Albany, setting off on their
journey West. They are looking for more,
fertile land to farm, taking everything
they own on the immensely precarious
trip. Their experience must reflect that of

Above: A wagon trail rolls westwards, but not all of the would-be settlers made it, and the trail was littered with sad memorials.

so many that started out on this perilous trek. They are afraid, but courageous, and excited by their new prospects.

But like so many other families that set off in the spirit of hopefulness, the Prescotts don't all make it West at this time, being obliged to settle where they are overtaken by hardship. In fact, it takes a couple of generations for the family to arrive in the Western lands.

For those that do make it West, L'Amour makes it clear that the same qualities and resilience demonstrated by the original settlers are needed to tame the new 'strange, lonely land.' The same mental readjustments are also required. Tracker and fur trader Linus Rawlings describes the negative reaction of many of the new settlers to the Western landscape, 'folks back east spent two hundred years learning how to pioneer in timber country, and when they first see the plains they call it a desert. It ain't nothing of the kind, just a different way of living, that's all.'

But despite the hardships, to many frontiers people, 'West was the magic word. It was the "Open Sesame" to fantastic futures.' Inevitably, not only the pure in heart were lured by the possibility of making their fortunes. Gamblers, cardsharps, land-grabbers, incorrigible villains, and women of uncertain virtue also followed the trail West. But just like the ocean voyages of the first white Americans, journeying to the West remained a metaphor for freedom and personal fulfilment. For others, it remained a flight from persecution. The Mormons, for example, to whom L'Amour refers on several occasions, make their pilgrimage to Utah in order to establish a settlement where they could practice their religious beliefs free from the discrimination they had met with in the East. The Mormon trek became legendary because so many of their number died en route, succumbing to the terrible conditions of their trek across the Rockies.

What the first people arriving in the West ultimately found was somewhat reminiscent of the East in the sixteenth

century. Fluid communities sprang up and died down just as quickly, when overtaken by misfortune: disease, Indian attack, or natural disaster.

But the sheer obduracy of the still-virgin territory and the hardness of the life it offered bred a plethora of fascinating characters for L'Amour to mine

Above: A romantic view of wagons in a rather well manicured wilderness.

Left: The conditions of the trek varied from bitter cold to extreme heat, and the terrain itself was invariably hostile.

Above: Snakes were just one of the many hazards faced by those trekking West.

Above and opposite page: The iconic wagon looks frail in the vast Western landscape.

in his fiction. As he said 'You cannot invent people like the real-life Molly Brown or the silver-mining baron Spencer Penrose who built his house in Virginia City, Nevada, with solid silver doorknobs throughout. They are all bigger than life and they did fantastic things… (and) these old characters were tough. If you

didn't shoot them they lived forever.' Their unforgettable alter egos flit through L'Amour's work, hundreds of different characters telling their fascinating stories and bringing an entire world back to life.

In their company, we can still make the journey West, in the footsteps of our guide and storyteller, Louis L'Amour.

Right: This wagon is equipped with a barrel of precious water.
Below: A marker stone commemorates the Oregon Trail, one of the famous routes to the West.

Bowie Knife

Above: Handmade Bowie knife with an 8 inch clip point blade and 'coffin-shaped' carved leather hilt with a brass pommel.

When times were tough and a man's gun and horse had been stolen or lost he always had his trusty Bowie knife to fall back on. Our introduction to Utah Blaine, after he has rescued Joe Neal from a lynch-mob, is as follows: Joe Neal says 'Where's your horse?'

Blaine replies, 'Don't have one.' The young man's possession's appeared to be nothing but the blankets and canteen. The flannel shirt he wore was ragged and sunfaded, the jeans did not fit him, and he had no hat. His only weapon was a Bowie knife with a bone handle.'

It is named for James Bowie, whose twin claims to fame were his death at the Alamo in 1836, and the imposing hunting and fighting knife that he carried.

Bowie was born in Kentucky in 1796, later moving to Louisiana where he engaged in the slave trade and land ventures. His reputation for fighting skills stemmed from a legendary brawl in 1827 known as the 'Sandbar Fight' in which he finished off his opponent with one thrust of 'a large butcher knife.' The fame of Bowie and his knife spread and soon men all over the expanding US territories were arming themselves in a similar manner.

Bowie has been the subject of many screen portrayals including being played by Richard Widmark in THE ALAMO [1960] and Scott Forbes in the TV series *The Adventures of Jim Bowie* [1956-58].

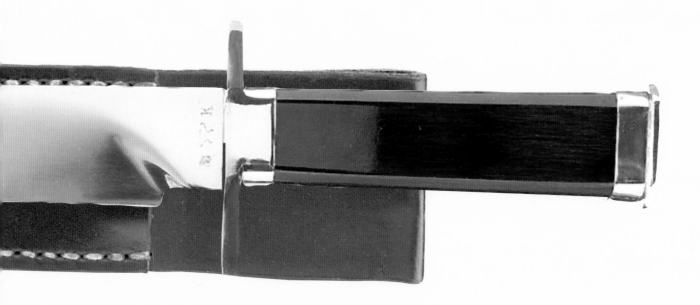

Above: The Classic Bowie blade
profile with the 'clip' point.

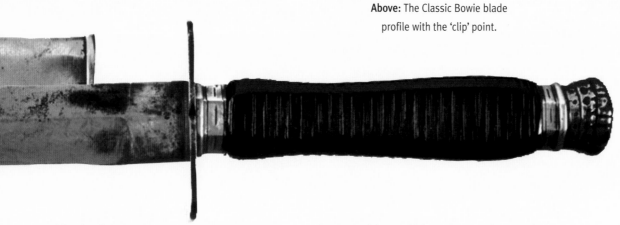

The knife, too, was awarded star status when the Warner Bros. props department created their own rather flashy version with a gold plated back edge to the blade and Jim Bowie's name on a brass plate on the handle, which couldn't have made for a comfortable grip in a tight corner. This version was used in a number of movies including THE ALAMO, Disney's DAVY CROCKETT, and the TV series.

Sadly, reality doesn't always live up to the legend, and when Jim Bowie died at the Alamo on the cold dawn of March 6th, 1836, he was suffering from typhoid fever and probably had little fight left in him as he raised himself from his sickbed to face the onrushing Mexican forces.

The legend has him dispatching a dozen enemy soldiers with his trusty blade.

Our example is a fairly workaday knife with a plain sewn leather scabbard such as L'Amour's characters would have carried. It has a 9 1/2 inch clip-point blade marked with an anvil and owners initials on the left side of the ricasso - the flat unbeveled part of the blade between the tang and the edged portion of the blade. It has a small extravagance – a silver cross guard and pommel. Silver decoration was popular in the West.

Mountain Men

'Every man in his life deserved one good dog and one good woman.' JIM BRIDGER

Below: Kit Carson and his fellow trappers gather around a roaring camp fire, to 'yarn' away the evening.

Louis L'Amour mentions several of the most famous of the mountain men in his work, and models several characters after them.

The original Western mountain men were members of the Ashley-Henry expedition of 1822. This was organized by the Rocky Mountain Fur Company in an attempt to break the fur-trading monopoly of the Hudson Bay Company. They met Cheyenne and Crow on their way West, and wisely learned all they could from them about trapping and surviving in the inhospitable climate. Perhaps the most famous of their number was twenty-three-year-old Jedediah Strong Smith, a Methodist storekeeper's son from New York State. His companions were obliged to sew his ear back on after an encounter with an enraged grizzly. He wore his hair long after this unfortunate incident.

Initially, the company was hugely successful, and the fur trade dominated the Rockies. The Rocky Mountain Fur Company arranged a unique method of collecting furs, where trappers met annually at pre-arranged 'Rendezvous' sites. The first was held in 1825 at Burnt Fork on the Green River, Wyoming. The

Most wore felt hats, buckskin jackets, leggings, and moccasins, and carried a Green River Butcher Knife and Plains Rifle or Flintlock. Almost half of them married Indian women, who helped them prepare the skins. Mountain

backbone of the industry was beaver pelts, as the felt hat industry demanded a huge number of these every year. The most famous of the mountain men also convened at these meetings, to trade furs and collect winter supplies, including Jim Bridger (who Linus Rawlings had known) and Kit Carson. Like Louis L'Amour characters Jethro Stuart and Osborne Russell, Carson had originally worked for the company, but left to become a free trapper, working for himself.

The typical mountain man that appeared at the Rendezvous often originated from the farms of the South or Midwest, and had become a trapper to share in this hugely profitable trade.

Above: Mountain men curing beaver pelts.

Left: Jim Beckwourth was another of the most notable mountain men. He was half African American.

Above: The essentials of a mountain man's life.

A Buffalo Hide covered water canteens with wooden stoppers.

B Possibles bag in Buffalo Hide.

C Handmade butcher knife, possibly Green River brand.

D Felt Hat with Buffalo Fur band.

E Pipe.

F Assortment of handmade horn tools.

G Horn Spoon.

H Powder horn.

I Buffalo fur gauntlets.

men were also tremendously active in blazing trails across the West, and were responsible for discovering the South Pass, known as the 'Great Gap of the Rocky Mountains.'

But the life of a mountain man was hard and dangerous, and hugely destructive to the wildlife of the West. They fell victim to grizzly attack, froze to death retrieving their traps from icy streams, were killed by Blackfeet, and succumbed to starvation. Survival could be almost worse, taking into account the appalling experiences that both Hugh Glass and John Coulter underwent after being attacked by the Blackfeet. All of this made them very tough indeed.

Left: Another convivial evening scene. Almost every man has a pipe to hand.

Far left: Mountain men bury their pelts in a cache by dead of night.

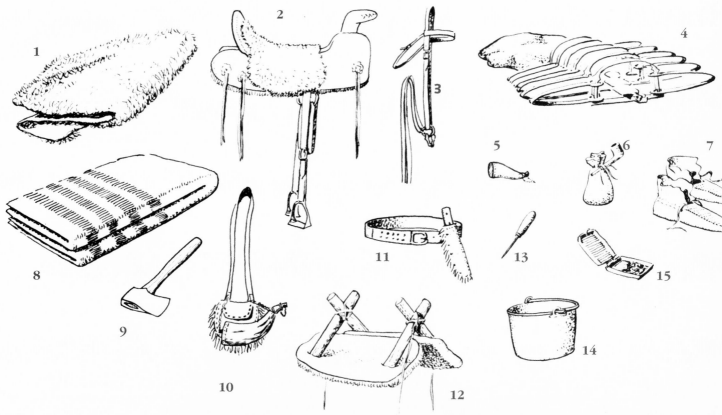

Above: Equipment:

1 Buffalo Hide Blanket.

2 Riding saddle.

3 Bear Trap.

4 Beaver Traps.

5 Powder Horn.

6 Tobacco sack and pipe.

7 Moccasins.

8 Indian Blanket.

9 Tomahawk.

10 Possibles bag.

11 Butcher knife in sheath on belt.

12 Pack Saddle.

13 Awl.

14 Iron Kettle.

15 Flints in striker box.

As Rowdy Jim Lowe says of mountain man Jethro Stuart, 'Talk soft around those old mountain men. You might kill one, but you'll have lead in you first. They die might hard – mighty hard indeed!'

By the time hat makers started to make silk top hats that didn't require pelts, the fur-bearing animals of the frontier had been all but exterminated. The Rocky Mountain Fur Company

Left: A typical mountain man costume of buckskin shirt and leggings.

collapsed in 1834, and most of the mountain men were obliged to take other forms of employment. By 1840, the year of the final Rendezvous, the fur trade was in terminal decline. Jim Bridger was obliged to hunt buffalo, and guide wagon trains through the vast territory that he and his ilk had helped to chart.

The very men who gloried in the Big Sky of the West, and its Shining Mountains had denuded it of its wildlife, and went back to the life of ordinary white men once they had taken their spoils.

Above: Mountain men needed speedy horses to outrun attacking Indians.

Left: Indian attack was one of the most serious hazards that beset the lives of the mountain men.

Remington Rolling Block Rifle

Below: The distinctive design of the Remington rifle clearly distinguishes it from other western arms.

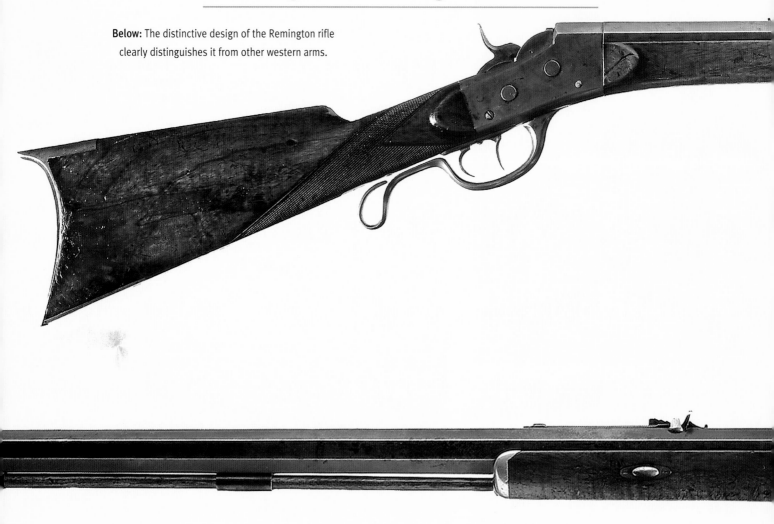

Above: A fine piece of gunsmithing from both Remington and Carlos Gove. Note the fancy touches like the silver fore end cap.

Lieutenant Colonel George Armstrong Custer was one of the larger than life character of the West. In HANGING WOMAN CREEK, Louis L'Amour tells us how Custer's troops cleaned up towns like Fargo-in-the Timber, 'Destroying local villains like Jack O 'Neil.'

Custer's time on the frontier with the US Cavalry was not just spent quelling Indians. He also took time off to go hunting in the Yellowstone National Park, where he used his favorite weapon, a Remington Rolling Block Sporting rifle. In a letter written to the Remington Company on October 5th, 1873 from his base at Fort Abraham Lincoln, Custer claimed that he killed far more game than all the other professional shots on the trip.

SPECIFICATIONS

Caliber: 0.40-.70 inch

Length of barrel: 30 inches

Barrel shape: Octagonal

Finish: Blue casehardened

Grips: Walnut

Action: Single shot/breech loading

Year of manufacture: 1874

Manufacturer: Remington/C. Gove & Co., Denver Armory, 340 Blake Street, Denver, Colorado

It is easy to think of rifles like the Winchester 1873 as the standard equipment for western shots but the Rolling Block rifle also made its mark. In the years following the Civil War, Remington was preoccupied with chasing lucrative military contracts, but many rifles were also sold to sportsmen and hunters. They were generally used for larger game, where a powerful, large caliber weapon was required. 'The Remington system' as it

This was a cheaper option as Allin was a government employee and the government could avoid paying a royalty to use the system.

But the US Navy did order significant quantities of Rolling Block rifles and carbines, and this contributed greatly to Remington's success. The Company must have been particularly pleased when a famed western hero and serving soldier like Custer praised their products.

Our featured gun has been converted to under-lever action by Carlos Gove, the pioneer Gun-maker of Denver, and has double set triggers. Carlos Gove rebuilt guns using this technique from 1873-77. The gun was handed down through a western family for several generations, having been given to Charlie Robbie, the original owner, for killing an Indian at the Sand Creek Massacre.

was correctly known, was developed by Joseph Rider as an improvement to his split breech concept, which was used on War models. The gun was a single shot breech – loader that would take a heavy charge center-fire cartridge, based on the design of army sharpshooter Colonel Hiram Berdan. Ultimately, however, the US Army decided in favor of rifles with the Allin 'trap door' action.

Above: Checkered stock and double set trigger show that this was a real shooter's gun.

Law and Order in the West

Outlaws and Lawmen

Throughout his work, Louis L'Amour makes it crystal clear that he believes the rule of law is the crux of civilization, without which society just can't function. The establishment of law and order is a fundamental theme that appears time and time again in Western literature, history, and film. Good men try to uphold the law, to protect the good and drive out the bad. As L'Amour says, 'here in these western lands men were fighting the age-old struggle for freedom and for civilization'. It's interesting that L'Amour often twins these two abstracts, which others (including many of his characters) see as being at odds.

But in enforcing a legal framework on a raw, new country, he also demonstrates that there is plenty of room for backsliding and ambiguity. The novels also show a good deal of friction between the 'law,' and 'right,' which often don't amount to the same thing. L'Amour tellingly portrays how the quality of the law often depends on the caliber of the law enforcer, and how even good law in the wrong hands can make for bad justice.

The young civilization of the West is often strongly contrasted to that of the Old World, and the Eastern US that the settlers have left behind. 'The trouble with most folks coming out here is that they've been protected so long they're no longer even conscious of it. Back where they come from there are rules and laws, curbstones and sidewalks, and policemen to handle violence. The result is that violence is no longer real for them.' This

naiveté leaves incomers pathetically vulnerable. As Barney Pike says of Ann Farley (in HANGING WOMAN CREEK), she 'wasn't long from England, and over there they have respect for the law, and let the law take its course, as should be done everywhere.' A lawless vacuum, with nothing to check the power of unscrupulous and self-interested men ends up costing her brother's life.

It's clear to Barney, that in the absence of the law, it is up to him to revenge Philo's murder and protect Ann: 'here in the West there sometimes wasn't much law, and there were some things the law and other folks preferred a man settle for himself.' Lesser men would fold under these dire pressures, but L'Amour's heroes call on their strength and self-reliance to do the right thing.

THE WILD, WILD WEST OF LOUIS L'AMOUR is packed full of courageous individualists who are more than capable of fighting their own battles. But L'Amour points out that, for a normal society to emerge in the 'beautiful country,' this just isn't enough. As Ben Cowan says in CATLOW, the West 'must be made safe for women and children. It must become a country to live in, not just a country to loot and leave… For that we need law, we need justice.' Ben is the voice of law in the book, which can be read as a brilliant

Opposite page: An early advertisement for Colt, one of the archetypal guns of the West.

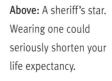

Above: A sheriff's star. Wearing one could seriously shorten your life expectancy.

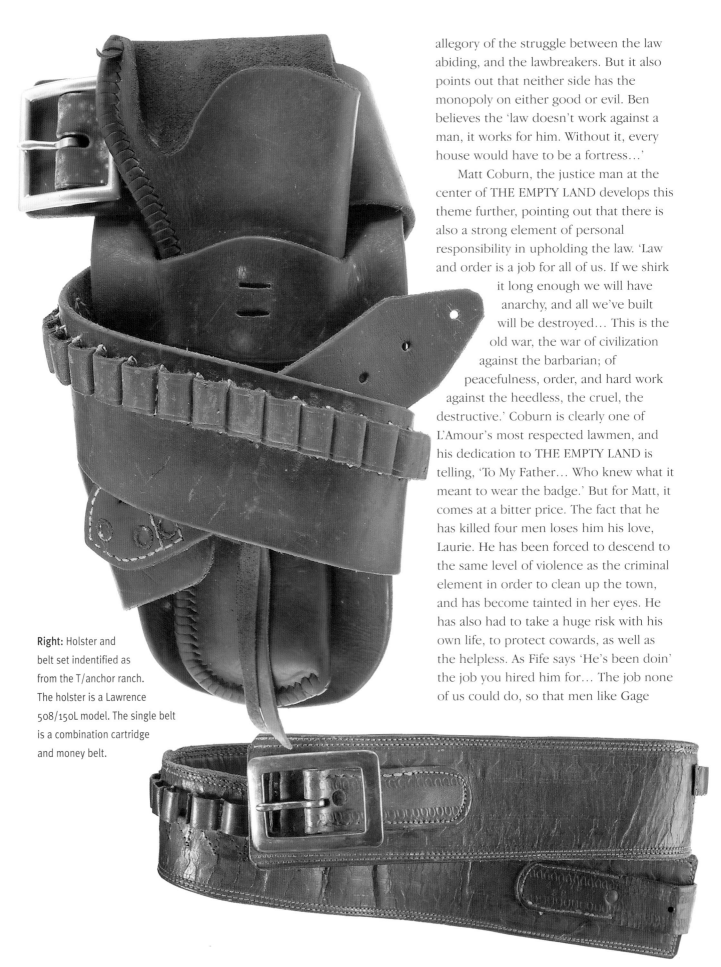

allegory of the struggle between the law abiding, and the lawbreakers. But it also points out that neither side has the monopoly on either good or evil. Ben believes the 'law doesn't work against a man, it works for him. Without it, every house would have to be a fortress…'

Matt Coburn, the justice man at the center of THE EMPTY LAND develops this theme further, pointing out that there is also a strong element of personal responsibility in upholding the law. 'Law and order is a job for all of us. If we shirk it long enough we will have anarchy, and all we've built will be destroyed… This is the old war, the war of civilization against the barbarian; of peacefulness, order, and hard work against the heedless, the cruel, the destructive.' Coburn is clearly one of L'Amour's most respected lawmen, and his dedication to THE EMPTY LAND is telling, 'To My Father… Who knew what it meant to wear the badge.' But for Matt, it comes at a bitter price. The fact that he has killed four men loses him his love, Laurie. He has been forced to descend to the same level of violence as the criminal element in order to clean up the town, and has become tainted in her eyes. He has also had to take a huge risk with his own life, to protect cowards, as well as the helpless. As Fife says 'He's been doin' the job you hired him for… The job none of us could do, so that men like Gage

Right: Holster and belt set indentified as from the T/anchor ranch. The holster is a Lawrence 508/150L model. The single belt is a combination cartridge and money belt.

(the gutless store keeper) can stay after all and 'feel safer now'.'

L'Amour is also quick to point out that not everyone with the frontier mentality welcomes the introduction of a judicial society. The West's very lawlessness was attractive to some. As Charlie Gant says to Zeb Rawlings, 'I don't like what you and your kind have done to this country… Used to be a man felt free around here, now a man can hardly breathe.' But L'Amour's portrayal of Gant as greedy and narrow-minded makes it pretty clear that his own sympathies lie with Zeb, who replies, 'I haven't noticed any honest men having trouble.' L'Amour also shows how the vacuum created by the lack of a justice system leads to strong individuals laying down a twisted 'law' of their own. The unscrupulous cattle baron, Ben Curry, lives likes a 'feudal lord and has no respect for any law he did not make himself.'

Zeb Rawlings also voices one of the other pillars of L'Amour's views on law enforcement, 'It will be necessary for the men of peace to have guns, as long as men of violence do. We can't put all the force in the hands of evil.' In fact, Louis L'Amour is pretty unambiguous that his heroes have the absolute right to bear arms, to defend themselves and others. The contemporary lawyer, William Blackstone, argued the legality of being able to 'repel force by force' in self-defense, and in the context of the time and place, it seems obvious to L'Amour that good people must be just as prepared to use force as wrongdoers are. As Eddie Holt tells his partner, Barney Pike, 'You're a kindly man, Pronto… but you can only be kindly up to a point, when you live in a world where evil men go armed.' In the real life West, there actually were a few pacifists, like Marshal 'Bear River' Tom Smith who refused to use their guns. Smith was axed to death by an angry homesteader.

Above: The Town Marshal's office also often served as the local jail. It showed that there was a local commitment to the forces of law and order.

But the novels also carry a strong sense that L'Amour is well aware that strength and power also have the capacity to corrupt. That even justified killing has consequences. Several of his heroes worry that the violence they are forced to use may reduce them to soulless 'killers.' Matt Coburn (THE EMPTY LAND) has made 'a dozen towns decent to live in' (according to Matt Sturd). But he fears that he is losing his patience, and will end up a professional killer. L'Amour describes how this fate can also happen to professional lawmen. In CATLOW, he tells

NO GUNS IN TOWN LIMITS
BY ORDER OF THE MARSHAL

MARSHAL

Left: Just as Wild Bill Hickok did in Abilene, and Rocky White did in Red Creek, this marshal has attempted to ban the carrying of guns within the town limits.

Both below: 'Autie' Custer and his men were responsible for cleaning up many Western towns, but also stirred up trouble from the dispossessed Indians (seen below plundering a hidden cache).

of Lynch Manly, a 'noted man-hunter and a man-killer who had once been a Royal Northwest Mounted policeman.' L'Amour women seem to know instinctively that 'turnin' bad' is a real hazard of this tough way of life. Though women like Laurie turn to strong men for protection, they can't necessarily accept what this entails.

The first organized law enforcement in the West was undertaken by the US army. They decriminalized many Western towns, including Fargo-in-the-Timber. L'Amour tells how 'Custer's soldiers cleaned it out,' despatching some of the local villains like Jack O'Neil. Unfortunately, 'Autie' was also responsible for stirring up attacks from burnt-out and dispossessed Indians, reduced to attacking settlers to survive. The Army was also employed by the railroad kings to protect their huge capital investment in schemes

like the transcontinental rail route. This is how Zeb Rawlings enters the scene in HOW THE WEST WAS WON as an army Lieutenant, protecting railroad workers from Arapahoe attack.

The first variety of 'citizens law' was an ugly and violent force, regulated by greed and self-interest rather than a desire to regulate frontier life. UTAH BLAINE opens with the attempted lynching of the elderly Joe Neal in a 'land grab' conspiracy, not by a 'committee of honest citizens but some dark and ugly bunch out to do business that demanded night and secrecy.' Utah Blaine himself is an example of just how easy it was to cross and re-cross the line of the law. He had been the Marshal of Alta, and had 'tamed' the town. He then became a mercenary fighter in the Mexican revolution, and ended up as a prisoner. Through hitching up with Joe Neal, he now becomes a man with a stake in society again, fighting the vigilante forces of the corrupt locals. He is a good example of a man with a reputation on both sides of the law.

Lynch law is a pretty common thread that runs through the novels. Nevers offers five hundred dollars for Utah Blaine, 'dead or alive.' Mercer threatens to take the law into his own hands, and hang Catlow as a cattle rustler. 'Hired guns' could be employed on either side of the criminal divide, depending on who hired them. Todd and Peebles are criminals and drunks, but other professional guns were more discriminating about their employers. Although Western men may be handy enough with a gun to solve their own difficulties, they are not necessarily interested in resolving other people's problems. As Barney Pike tells Granville Stuart, when the rancher tries to hire him to clean up a plague of cattle rustlers (in HANGING WOMAN CREEK) 'when it comes to the law, I leave it to the law… I'm not a man-hunter.'

The first sheriffs and marshals were often directly employed by the local townspeople and landowners to 'clean up' their towns and the surrounding lands, leaving them to live and do their business in peace. This brought a gradual drift towards professionalism, and the use of more recognizable policing methods. For example, L'Amour describes how the violent and disruptive Range Wars finally drive the townspeople of Red Creek to get their own marshal, Rocky White. His job is to ensure that 'the violence stops, guns (are) checked upon entry of the town limits…' that there is 'protection for citizens.' This system was obviously open to abuse, and the hard nature of the work meant that the men employed to do it were often distasteful to their employers. A well-known real life example of this is that of Wild Bill Hickok, who brought law, order, and gun control to Abilene, only to be sacked by the town council for his unsavory and violent methods.

In THE EMPTY LAND, Matt Coburn suggests that Confusion should employ a rough and ready brand of law

Above: Vigilantes bring in an outlaw. There is probably a reward posted for him. L'Amour heroes are often ambiguous about this kind of 'man-hunting.'

Right: Cattle rustling and range wars were constant problems for cattle ranchers during this period. They often led to violence, but were often outside the scope of the local lawmen.

Above: Deputy sheriffs could be appointed *ad hoc* in times of crisis.

Opposite Page: Wyeth's magnificent painting celebrates 'The Noble Outlaw.' But in reality, men of this type were often violent and depraved.

enforcement, effectively vigilantism; a citizens committee enforcing the law with Winchesters and an 'uplift society… use a rope to do the lifting.' But his employer, Felton, says that the town wants to see an end to violence, and that there 'just has to be another way.' The relationship between the townspeople and their 'hired law' was often full of irony. Felton considers Coburn to be little better than a gunfighter, but Coburn insists that he has 'never hired my gun to anybody but the law.' In fact, he had once dreamt of becoming a lawyer, and bought a copy of 'Blackstone,' the famous legal textbook. He finally accepts the job as Sheriff of Confusion after the first man to be offered the position (McGuiness) is shot dead, and the second, 'thief and high-binder' Hick Sutton is ridden out of town. L'Amour describes Coburn's increasing weariness at the task. He had initially found rough new towns like Confusion interesting – a challenge. 'He had come to them to bring law and order… but all

too often he had discovered that even those who hired him became his enemies' and he goes on to describe how 'a man in my line of work doesn't have too many friends.' Despite the huge risks he and his kind take to 'clean up,' and enforce justice, they receive very little gratitude and are often lonely and isolated.

Two town marshals who L'Amour created and admired, Borden Chantry and Tyrel Sackett, appear in SON OF A WANTED MAN (Tyrel also appears in several Sackett saga novels). They both espouse the aspirations of real life lawman Dave Cook, who brought a new level of professionalism to the role. They follow his precept of cooperation between lawmen, in tracking criminals down and bringing them to justice (as the Texas Rangers did). Cook believed that 'Any town marshal worth his salt could in a few minutes detect the presence of strangers, of lone riders, or drifters, even in a town that was strange to him.' Chantry very modestly describes himself as being 'no detective or even a marshal except by wish of these folks in town.' In fact, he is both the town marshal and county sheriff, drawing the

Above: The legendary Judge Roy Bean dispensed justice from The Jersey Lilly in Langtry, Texas. There is a museum to commemorate his influence on the town.

salary for both jobs. He is a completely honest and incorruptible man, impervious to bribery, 'I'm not for sale. An officer who turns crooked is worse than any thief. A police officer takes an oath to support the law.' He feels satisfaction when he, Sackett, and Kim Baca have wiped out the outlaw band coming to rob the town bank, 'This was his town, and it was safe once more.' But this safety for the citizens was bought at a tremendously high price, and only because men of his stamp were willing to take such huge personal risks. Chantry, and men of his caliber, are truly 'mighty square.' Another man of this ilk is Zeb Rawlings. He resigns his army commission goes into civilian law enforcement and ultimately becomes a

Deputy US Marshal. He is known 'as a man who was never anxious to shoot, which was rare in old-time marshals who had grown into their jobs at a time when it was often safer to shoot first and ask the questions afterwards.' He is brave and self-disciplined. Like Chantry and Sackett, Rawlings also believes that lawmen must cooperate to get better results, and use modern 'technology' to track down criminals. 'The law was organized now. Descriptions were mailed around from office to office, and conceit (on the part of the lawbreakers) led to carelessness… imprisonment or death.'

In HOW THE WEST WAS WON, Louis L'Amour very interestingly categorizes three types of frontier marshal.

Courageous and restrained men like Zeb Rawlings, in the stamp of real life lawmen such as Bill Tilghman, Jim Gillette, and Jeff Milton; a second type as personified by Bill Hickok who 'gave you no second chance'; then a third kind of man, exemplified by Mysterious Dave Mather who proactively went looking for troublemakers. Men like this 'shot you where they found you' – if you were on the wrong side of the law, of course. Inevitably, this meant that the personality of the lawmen was reflected in the quality of the law dispensed in these towns, which must have been pretty variable.

But the law gradually became more codified, and law enforcement itself more uniform and professional. On the other hand, criminals seem to have become more hardened and depraved. Western society itself became far less tolerant of the blight of lawlessness. L'Amour describes how, in the past, an outlaw might have been seen as 'some wild youngster full of liquor,' but would now be considered 'a bad man, dangerous to the community.' L'Amour sums up the situation by saying 'To defend against the kind of outlaws I write about... as the towns of the western frontier began to develop... there was a great need for law enforcement officials to become more professional.' This professional approach, and the better results it produced, greatly reduced vigilantism. More criminals were sent to prison, rather than being summarily strung up, so a prison service was also established. Finn Cagle is described as having served a term in Yuma's Territorial Prison.

While L'Amour's portrayal of Western lawmen is often admiring, he seems a good deal less impressed by lawyers (his evocations of them are far more variable) and members of the judiciary. Dean Cullane was a 'jackleg lawyer, and one who dealt with men on the wrong side of the law in ways not concerned with the legal profession.' But Judge Niland (THE

MAN CALLED NOON) must be a candidate for the most corrupted man of law in the novels. He offers Ruble Noon the opportunity to rob Fan Davidge of her inheritance, and incites him to

Above: 'Mysterious' Dave Mather, a new breed of law officer who would go looking for trouble, and 'shot you where they found you.'

The Age of the Gunfighter

The gunfighter fills a special place in the folklore of the American West, alongside the cowboy, Indian, mountain man, scout, and sheriff. His image is still fresh in the mind, although over a century has passed since he squeezed a trigger. But like many Western characters, his figure evokes conflicting feelings, for men of this type ranged all the way from being 'man-killers' through to 'civilizers.' Louis L'Amour had met many men of the class, and he was clearly fascinated by them, having written profiles of thousands more. He attempts to explain their position to the reader, 'Few gunfighters were actually outlaws… A gunfighter, or gunman, was actually no more than a man who, because of some unusual gift of dexterity, coordination, and nerve, became better with a gun than others.' But evidently, he himself had ambiguous feelings about men of this stamp. Some of his gunmen are cold, contract killers, others are depraved and vicious, 'thoroughly bad men' while yet others are more 'gentlemen thieves,' like the 'Admirable Outlaw' in N.C. Wyeth's painting. Often, they were law enforcers (like the real life Bat Masterson and Bill Tilghman, on whom Zeb Rawlings is based), and standing indomitably on the side of right. Yet another class of gunman, like the often-mentioned 'Wild' Bill Hickok and the Earp brothers, were economically motivated. They used their gun skills to find work between other

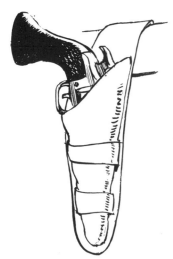

Right: Western Heiser Holster with belt. The two loop holster is marked with the straight 'Heiser Denver' mark.

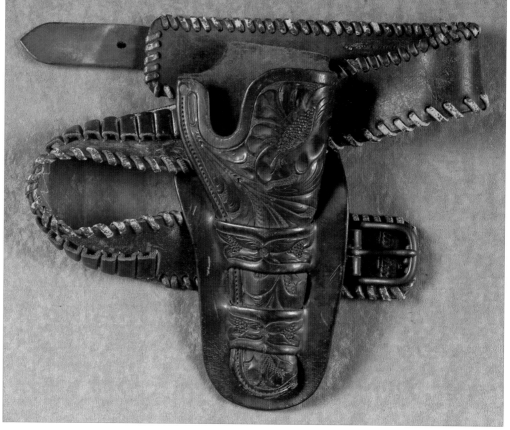

Below: Professional gunfighters and law enforcers were often difficult to tell apart in the hurly burly of the wild, wild West. Speed of the draw was everything for both classes. Without it, a marshal's badge was no protection.

jobs, often 'taking the badge' of a law officer. Other men, like Utah Blaine, were more 'unofficial' gunfighters, using their modus operandi to achieve their own ends. He is variously described as a 'hell-on-wheels gunman from the Neuces,' a 'ragged-tailed gunslinger' and 'damned driftin' outlaw.'

In HOW THE WEST WAS WON, L'Amour composes a fascinating profile of the hugely diverse backgrounds that these men came from: 'Most gunfighters had been officers of the law… Hickok had been a stagedriver and scout for the army. Wyatt Earp, Bat Masterson, Billy Brooks, and many others had been buffalo

Right: Fancy tooled leather holster and belt for a Colt Army Revolver.

Below: Fine Texas holster stamped J.D.Banks/Amarillo/Texas.

Above: Combination cartridge and belt with 35 large caliber, cartridge

Above: Buscadero fancy holster rig. Twin holsters in tooled leather for a pair of Colt Peacemakers.

Below: Small Western belt with 3/8 inch plated brass tacks.

Below: Cartridge belt and holster for Colt Single action.

hunters; Clay Allison, Pink Higgins, and John Slaughter had been ranchers, Ben Thompson a gambler, Doc Holliday a dentist, Temple Houston a lawyer. Billy the Kid had been a drifting cowhand and gambler, then a feudist in the Lincoln County War…Chris Madsen had been a soldier in several armies… Buckey O'Neill was a newspaper editor, probate judge, and a superintendent of schools, as well as a frontier sheriff; many gunfighters have been ex-soldiers.' Many other famous names also turn up in L'Amour's pages, including Frank and George Coe, Dick Brewer, Jesse Evans, and Wes Hardin. Ben Curry's 'bunch of outlaws' (in SON OF A WANTED MAN) recalls real life outfits like the Dalton Gang.

L'Amour's version very much reflects contemporary accounts of the gunman phenomenon. A sketch in a similar vein appeared in the *Kansas City Journal* in 1881, 'The gentleman who has 'killed his man' is by no means a rara avis… He is met daily on Main street… He may be seen on 'change, and in the congregations of the most aristocratic churches. He resides on 'Quality Hill,' or perhaps on the East Side… He may be found behind the bar in a Main street saloon… or he may be behind the rosewood counters of a bank.' But men who lived and died by the gun as a profession were an exception to the rule, even in THE WILD, WILD WEST OF LOUIS L'AMOUR.

In reality, the gunfighter emerged from the turbulent conditions prevalent in the frontier West, when little or no help could be expected from the law. Men like Matt Giles started out with respectable backgrounds but are sucked into the way of the gun by the forces of history, beginning 'his killing as mere boy in the Moderators and Regulators wars of northeast Texas, and had graduated to a sharpshooter in the Confederate Army.' He describes Pike Sides, the 'Cherry Creek Gunman' in THE EMPTY LAND, who came to killing via a similar route,

Right: Gunfighter's Heiser shoulder holster marked H.H. Heiser/Maker/ Denver/Colo.

'God created man, but Sam Colt made them equal!'

Right: Sam Colt was a major firearms manufacturer, and became a huge asset to the Union cause in the Civil War, supplying them with many different models.

Right: Although not created during Sam Colt's actual lifetime, the Single Action Revolver was one of the company's finest products during the frontier years, and along with the Winchester 1873 Rifle, became known as 'the gun that won the West.'

having been involved in the Lincoln County War, and was subsequently hired to slaughter several men around the west. L'Amour obviously disapproves of this kind of 'cold' contract killing; he describes Pike as having 'curiously unalive (eyes), reminding Matt of a snake.'Pike's soul is dead.

In the alternative moral order of the West, one of the lowest forms of 'gunman' that turns up in the novels is Eve Rawlings's sickly younger brother Zeke (now known as Ralls) in HOW THE WEST WAS

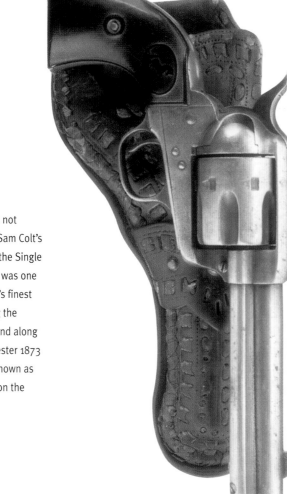

WON. This is a case of a very bad apple coming from a good barrel, and L'Amour interestingly describes how a boy from a good, loving family (that has also turned out men of the stature of Zeb Rawlings), has turned into a 'particularly vicious killer.' Zeke is a thoroughly bad man who never did a day's work in his life. He doesn't even espouse the virtue of honor amongst thieves. He abandoned his own gang to be hung in Jack Slade's cleanup, when vigilantes accounted for the deaths of twenty-six outlaws who had been terrorizing their town – Virginia City, Montana. Even outlaws had their standards, the lowest of the low being referred to as 'scalp hunters' and 'back-shootin' killers.' Most would be appalled to learn of Zeke's intention to murder a relative, although he does attempt to justify this, by explaining that the elderly Jethro Stuart isn't blood kin.

One positive aspect of the prominence of gunmen in the Western environment was the tremendous affect it had on the manufacture of ever more sophisticated guns. Samuel Colt patented the revolver in 1835, which was a huge step forward in automatic firing. Some men said that 'God created man, but Sam Colt made them equal!' Many Louis L'Amour heroes and villains carry Colts of several different kinds, Spencer .56 revolving shotguns, .45s and .44s. Winchesters are also rated, and appear just as often (.45s, 73s etc.). In THE MAN CALLED NOON, Ruble Noon is trying to recover his memory and his identity, and discovers that he was the president and owner of an arms company, a famous marksman, and big game hunter. Interestingly, he carries a Winchester. The English Daily Telegraph remarked in 1869 that 'Duellists, travellers, and the rowdy bullies of the New World enjoy the doubtful honor of having brought the pistol to its present sanguinary perfection.

It is the weapon of the self-dependent man.' This weapon was indeed one of the factors that helped to 'win' the West for white men.

But in some L'Amour's novels, there is also a sense that the true day of the gunman is drawing to a close. Ben Curry articulates this feeling: 'All of us… Wyatt Earp, Billy the Kid, Bill Hickok, we've all lived out our time in a world we never made.' Progress, and the incoming force of law are sweeping these men aside, together with the wilderness itself.

Below: A Fancy Buscadero holster rig with double buckle belt decorated with brass tacks. A single cartridge belt. A single holster for a Colt Peacemaker with leather thong, which tied the assembly to the gunfighters leg for a faster draw.

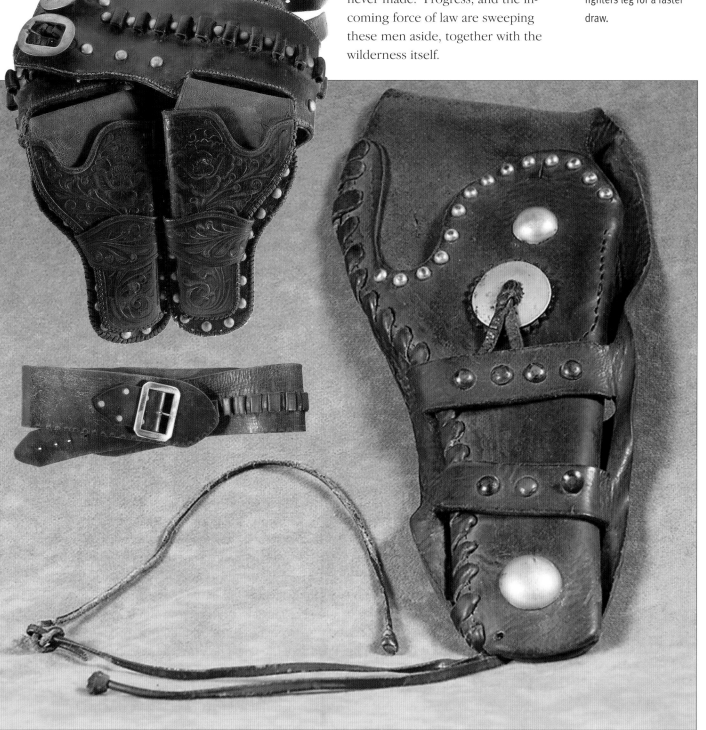

Colt Peacemaker

The gun shown here was the property of the Sheriff of Magdalena, New Mexico. The gun is shown with what is believed to be its original leather tooled holster.

No weapons appraisal of the West of Louis L'Amour could be considered complete without the Peacemaker, or Single Action Army Revolver as it was more properly called. Along with the Winchester 73, the Colt Peacemaker became famous as 'the gun that won the west.' Both Models were deliberately marketed to use the same ammunition, typically either .44/40 or .45 inch caliber. This meant that it was only necessary to carry one type of shell, a self-contained center fire cartridge. The two guns presented the all round flexibility of a repeating rifle for long-range work, with the quick shot revolver for use at short range. Both had outstanding stopping power, provided by the large caliber ammunition.

In HANGING WOMAN CREEK, 'Pronto' Pike is presented with both guns by his new employer, Bill Justin, as part of a wagon load of essential supplies: 'two brand-new Winchester 73s, and boxes with about 500 rounds of ammunition. Alongside the rifles lay two .44 caliber Colts, both new.

This image of the cowboy carrying both weapons as part of his outfit was promoted by Hollywood. But the Colt was tremendously expensive at $17 (around $700 today). Back in 1874, this would have been around a

vision for revolving firearms propelled the company forward for many years after his death. After all, as the popular saying went, 'God made man, but Colonel Colt made them equal.'

month's wages for the average cowhand. It might not have been all that prevalent.

But the Colt .45 Peacemaker was a familiar part of John Wayne's screen image, and when he starred in the screen version of HONDO, the image stuck. The gun became the model that all toy guns were based on – my own nickel-plated die cast version was a personal childhood favorite – as it was with countless millions of other kids that grew up in the golden age of Westerns.

Ironically, the gun was not the direct result of Samuel Colt's own design as he died in 1862. This was before the advent of the type of ammunition that made the 1873 revolver so effective. But it can certainly be argued that Colt's powerful

The featured example was the property of the Sheriff of Magdalena New Mexico. It has its original handmade single loop holster, decorated with brass tacks and braided rawhide edging. Many guns of this type have been handed down in families for generations.

SPECIFICATIONS

Caliber: 0.45 inch

Length of barrel: 4 inches

Barrel shape: Round

Finish: Smooth gray patina with traces of blue

Grips: Hard Rubber

Action: Single

Year of manufacture: 1896

Manufacturer: Colt's PT.F.A. MFG. CO., Hartford, Connecticut

Gambling

Opposite page: A tin type photograph of four men playing cards.

Gambling was a major ingredient in the cocktail of Western life. 'A mania for gambling' was common to all the frontier regions, and it was the chief draw of saloon life. Most gamblers were parasitic. They migrated to wherever there was money, in the mining and cow towns, or the tent towns at the end of the railroad tracks. In these places, gambling and prostitution formed a corrosive mix

was also reckoned among its most respectable.' Gaming certainly attracted many professional players, including many of the West's most famous gunmen.

Several of Louis L'Amour's most colorful characters are also gamblers. Not one is successful. As Lilith Van Valen says, 'A man's a fool to gamble, take that from me, who was married to a gambler. But you'd best know how, because there

Right: A typical card deck of the 1880s showing 53 saucily clad actresses.

Below: A gambler's cane. It's ivory top contains three dice in a silver plated canister.

that greatly increased the level of violence. Towns like Abilene tried to control the activities of the 'pasteboard pirates' with a stringent system of fines, but its own Marshal, Bill Hickok, was a professional gambler who ran the town from a saloon table. Indeed, Bat Masterson wrote that 'gambling was not only the principle and best-paying industry of the town at the time, but it

might come a time.' When she met him, her husband Cleve was a washed up riverboat gambler, whose luck had run out. And in any case, as Barney Pike says, 'Gamblin' money don't stick to a man.' He himself is penniless, despite winning $300 in a Chicago dice game.

Other characters, like Doc Sawyer, use gambling to collect saloon intelligence. He later cheats, by card marking, in a game he plays with Ben Curry and Garlin. 'You shuffle them cards any more, Doc... and I'll get worried what you're doin' to that deck.' Cheats and 'short-card artists'

Left and Above: Top hat with cheaters mirror in the crown.

Below: Gamblers dirk, which would have been clipped inside a waistband for cutting one's way out of a tight corner.

Gambling was one of the darker threads that ran through Western life.

were also instrumental in cranking up the level of gun fighting in Western towns. The Abilene Chronicle published a whole list of well-known card tricks and cheating methods for their more 'respectable' readers to watch out for.

Mike Bastian also pretends to have an (unlikely) interest in 'draw poker' to

explain his appearance in the saloon to the Sheriff of Weaver. At the other end of the moral spectrum, outlaw and thief Charlie Gant seems to indicate the depths of his debauchery by setting up a roulette wheel. Gunman Wyatt Earp made his fortune doing this very thing.

Above: Two fine riverboats which were actually floating magnets to the gambling fraternity.

Left: Highly ornate poker chips from the frontier days.

Smith & Wesson .44 Russians

Below: Intricate engraving complements the S&W trademark in brass set into the walnut handgrip.

Utah Blaine is holed up at the hotel in Red Creek when he notices a man staring up at his window outside in the street. There is something sinister in his fixed scrutiny.

Blaine turns from the window and he opens a carpetbag and to take out a pair of holsters and a wide gun belt. 'He slung the belt around him and buckled it, then he took from the bag two beautifully matched pistols. They were .44 Russians. He checked their loads, then played with them briefly, spinning them, doing a couple of border shifts, and then dropping them into their holsters. Suddenly, his hands flashed and the guns were in his hands.'

The .44 Russians were in fact Smith & Wesson No 3 Model Army revolvers. The guns got their nomenclature, as they were part of a massive order from the Russian authorities, which absorbed Smith & Wesson's entire manufacturing capacity for a full five years. The gun was manufactured around a special .44 inch cartridge specified by the Russian Army. This cartridge gave it excellent power and made the gun a serious rival to Colt's equivalent models of the 1870s. The design evolved into the double-action 1881 Frontier Revolver, which started to show the lines we recognize in the modern Magnum.

The No 3 Model remained in production for many years. This example has been engraved after leaving the factory. This was not unusual. The dark blue/black casehardened finish of the barrel cylinder and frame contrasts beautifully with the engraving, which is filled in with gilt to set it off. It is both fancy and deadly at the same time. A brace of these revolvers in a pair of holsters were serious equipment for the western gunfighter.

Right: Unlike Colt, the whole barrel and chamber assembly folded down to load. Note the intricate pattern around the pivot pin.

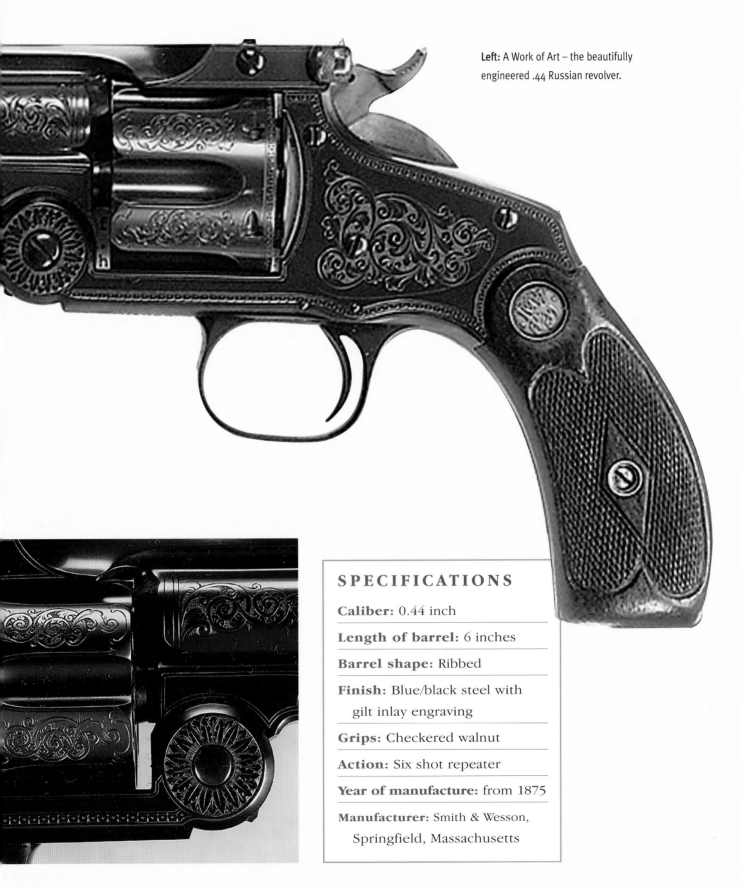

Left: A Work of Art – the beautifully engineered .44 Russian revolver.

SPECIFICATIONS

Caliber: 0.44 inch

Length of barrel: 6 inches

Barrel shape: Ribbed

Finish: Blue/black steel with gilt inlay engraving

Grips: Checkered walnut

Action: Six shot repeater

Year of manufacture: from 1875

Manufacturer: Smith & Wesson, Springfield, Massachusetts

Gunfighter Profiles

Wyatt Berry Stapp Earp
1848-1929

Below: Wyatt Earp at the most famous shoot-out of all time, the O. K. Corral in Tombstone, where the three Earp brothers swapped lead with the Clanton-McLaury gang. They survived, but some of their opponents were not so lucky. Frank and Tom McLaury fell, as did Billy Clanton.

Wyatt Earp was born in Monmouth, Illinois, and grew up on an Iowa farm. He became one of the most complex and interesting of the gunfighter frontiersmen of the West.

In 1864, Wyatt and his brothers moved to Colton, California, with their parents (which is near San Bernadino). He took various jobs, working as a shotgun messenger for Wells Fargo, a railway worker, and a buffalo hunter. Like Bill Hickok, he also worked in law enforcement to boost his career, serving as deputy marshal in Wichita, Kansas, and in Dodge City. He was reputed to have carried a Colt handgun, either an Army or a Peacemaker. Less reliably, legend has it that he used a Colt 'Buntline Special,' with a detachable carbine. But this

particular weapon may have been presented to him in the 1920s, by an admiring fan. Personally, Earp was noted as a tough and decisive man, but was also considered by many to be a 'cold fish.' Despite this, he became lifelong friends with Bat Masterson and Doc Holliday during this Kansas period. Like many of his kind, he also gained a reputation as a professional gambler.

Earp had returned East and married in 1870, but his new wife died suddenly. He remarried, and left Dodge City in 1878, setting up home with his brothers and their wives in Tombstone, Arizona. In dress and manner, the Earp brothers exemplified the typical gunmen of the time, poised and stylish. Wyatt acquired the gambling concession in the Oriental

Saloon, and his brother Virgil became town marshal. Brother Morgan worked for the local police department. Earp's second marriage failed, and he met his third wife, Josephine Marcus in Tombstone. But everything in Tombstone wasn't rosy. A feud developed between the Earps and Ike Clanton's gang that culminated in 1881 with the most famous gunfight of them all, outside the O.K. Corral, where the Earp brothers 'swapped lead' with the Clanton-McLaury gang. The three Earp bothers survived, but a fourth brother, Morgan, was gunned-down by an unknown assassin in the following year. The remaining brothers avenged his death, and Wyatt was obliged to skip town to Colorado to avoid being tried for these revenge killings.

But Earp remained a law enforcer, of sorts. In 1893, he became of member of the so-called 'Dodge City Peace Commission' (together with men such as Bat Masterson and Charlie Bassett), which convened to support fellow gunslinger and saloon owner Luke Short. The city fathers of Dodge City wanted to clean up the town and make it more attractive to settlers, so they tried to evict undesirable elements like Short and his ilk. They soon backed down when Luke's friends turned up.

Wyatt and Josie spent the next few years tramping around the booming mining towns of the frontier, gambling and investing in real estate and saloons as they passed through. In 1897, they operated a saloon in Alaska at the peak of the gold rush there, and made a fortune

Above: The Dodge City Peace Commission of 1883. Back *(left to right)*: Harris, Short, Masterson, W.F. Petillon (added later to the genuine photograph). Front: C. E. Bassett, Wyatt Earp, M.F. Mclain, and Neil Brown. The 'Commission' assembled to support fellow gunslinger Luke Short.

Above: Wyatt Earp's Oriental Saloon in Tombstone. This was one of his first investments in property and real estate.

mine for $30,000. He struck gold and copper in 1906 and spent the final winters of his life working these veins. He and Josie lived in Los Angeles in the summer, mixing with the Hollywood glitterati of the time.

Wyatt died in Los Angeles in 1929, at the ripe old age of 80. He was one of the very few gunslingers to make it into old age, and perhaps unique in that he was able to enjoy his own burgeoning reputation. He was an intensely paradoxical man, one who had both upheld and manipulated the law: a speculator and gambler, who was also an able businessman and investor who knew the value of hard work. He was a loyal friend and partner, who also inspired great devotion from his friends, but also noted for his cool demeanor and lack of personal warmth.

Like all the old gunslingers, he had his tricks of the trade. Earp claimed that he only ever loaded five bullets into a six-shooter to 'ensure against accidental discharge.'

estimated at $80,000. They then headed for Tonopah, Nevada, cashing in on that town's gold strike.

Earp ultimately took up prospecting seriously, and staked many claims in the Mojave Desert, including several just outside Death Valley. At one stage, he was reputed to have sold a worked-out silver

John 'Doc' Holliday
—— *1851-1887* ——

John 'Doc' Holliday was unusual amongst the gunfighters, good and bad, in that he came from a well-to-do background. He was born in Griffin, Georgia to Henry Burroughs Holliday and Alice Jane Holliday, and was their eldest surviving child. Henry Burroughs Holliday was a Confederate Major in the Civil War, and was later elected Major of Valdosa, Georgia. But misfortune came quickly, John was intensely close to his mother, but she died in 1866. To compound his loss, his father remarried within an indecently hasty three months.

Soon after he gained his degree qualifying him as a Doctor in Dental

Surgery from the Pennsylvania College of Dental Surgery in Philadelphia, a second blow fell. He was diagnosed with tuberculosis. Effectively, he spent the balance of his life on borrowed time, and this may have accounted for the extremely cavalier way he led it.

He had begun to practice dentistry in various Western boomtowns, including Dodge City, but his illness necessitated a move west to hotter, drier climates. By now, he was too ill to follow his profession, so he headed west to Dallas, and like so many men of his type, he became a professional gambler. Fellow gunman Bat Masterson, and unequivocal

Left: 'Doc' Holliday and his lady love, 'Big nose' Kate turned up in many Western boom towns, including Dodge City, Tucson, and Tombstone. He died young, ravaged by alcohol and tuberculosis.

Below: Holliday began his professional life as a dentist, but when he discovered that he was terminally ill, he decided to follow a more glamorous career as a professional gambler and gunman.

good guy (also mentioned by L'Amour), later described Doc as being of a 'mean disposition and an ungovernable temper, and under the influence of liquor was a most dangerous man.' His unpleasant temper and vagabond lifestyle resulted in a corrosive cocktail of violence and murder. He went about armed with a gun in a shoulder holster, a gun on his hip and a long, wicked knife. His long list of killings started with the murder of a local gambler in Dallas, and a pattern of 'kill

DENTISTRY.
J. H. Holliday, Dentist, very respectfully offers his professional services to the citizens of Dodge City and surrounding country during the summer. Office at room No. 24, Dodge House. Where satisfaction is not given money will be refunded.

and run' established itself so that Doc never felt safe in any one place for too long. The most foolish murder he committed was that of a soldier from Fort Richardson, which brought him to the attention of the US Government. Doc escaped, but now had a price on his head, and was wanted by the law. He moved to Denver, remaining almost anonymous until he slashed a gambler, Bud Ryan, and almost killed him. At this time, he also became involved with the only woman that came into his life, 'Big nose' Kate. 'Big nose' was a madam and prostitute who worked in these professions by choice. She was also one of the most famous of the gunwomen of the West, and an excellent shot. Although she and Doc attempted to live together respectably, the bright saloon lights were her natural habitat, and she returned to them time after time. Their relationship lasted, on and off, for many years, but was always volatile. On one occasion, 'Big nose' sprang Doc from jail in Fort Griffin, but when their relationship soured, she just as quickly turned him in.

The pattern of Doc's life was now set. Effectively, he was a professional killer. He rode with Wyatt Earp for some time, adding to his murder tally. In fact, one of his few redeeming features was his deep sense of loyalty to his friends, and to Earp in particular. Earp described him as a 'most skilful gambler, and the nerviest, fastest, deadliest man with a six-gun I ever saw.' But although Wyatt valued Holliday, he was also embarrassed by his behavior.

Although Doc claimed he had escaped nine attempts on his life – five ambushes and four hangings – he finally died in bed in Glenwood Springs, Colorado. His failing health had led him to this health resort, to try the sulphur spring water. He was just thirty-six years old, but contemporary accounts described his body as being so ravaged by drink and illness that he looked like a man of eighty. He took to his bed for 57 days, and was delirious for fourteen of them. Considering his style of life, this was a very strange way for him to die. His final words referred to this: 'This is funny,' he said.

The Dalton Gang

Opposite page, below: The Condon Bank at Coffeyville, from a contemporary photograph. This was the second target (the first being the First National Bank) of the Dalton gang's raid on their hometown, which went so disastrously awry.

Lewis and Adeline Dalton had a large family of fifteen children: ten boys and five girls. Most were born in Cass County, Michigan, where Lewis owned a saloon, but the family later settled on a farm outside of Coffeyville, Kansas. With no hint of what was to come, the eldest son, Frank, became a Deputy US Marshal, working in the dangerous Indian Territory. His younger brothers revered him, and the whole family were devastated when he was cruelly murdered. His younger brothers, Emmett, Grat, and Bob followed him into the service, but were soon disillusioned. Emmett described the work that was expected of them, 'Grafting as we of

today know the term was a mild, soothing description of what occurred.' There was also some disagreement over unpaid expenses, and the brothers quit. They subsequently became involved in a little cattle rustling, and became outlaws, working on the wrong side of the law. This is a pattern that L'Amour often describes. The penalties for minor wrongdoing were so draconian that there was no way back for the perpetrators, and they were almost obliged to lead a life of crime. This is what happened to the Daltons.

They began a brief but flamboyant career of robberies and holdups, ultimately planning to break all records by

pulling-off a double bank hoist in their hometown of Coffeyville. This was their first mistake. They rode into town, armed with pearl handled Colt .45s, disguised as a US Marshal and his posse. But the Dalton brothers were almost instantly recognized by a passerby, who alerted the marshal and townsfolk.

They had planned to rob the First National in the first place, and then go on to the Condon Bank. The first raid went off successfully, but as they left the Condon Bank, they were met by a hail of bullets from a group of armed citizens led by Marshal Charles T. Connelly. A massive gun battle ensued, in which Connelly and three townspeople were killed. After Connelly's demise, liveryman John J. Kloeher took over the attack and four members of the Dalton gang fell, shot in what is now known as Death Alley: Bob and Grat Dalton, Bill Powers and Dick Broadwell. Emmett was very

Above: The ignominious end of the Dalton Gang. The corpses of Brat and Bob Dalton Bill Powers, and Dick Broadwell, laid out like trophies outside the Coffeyville jail on October 5, 1892. They are handcuffed, even in death.

seriously wounded but miraculously survived. The bodies of the dead gang members were treated with scant regards, photographed like trophies, and publicly displayed. For years, they lay in a grave unmarked, except for a rusty piece of iron pipe to which the gang had tethered their horses. Emmett erected a headstone some years later. He himself served fourteen years in the Kansas State Penitentiary, and went on to lead a blameless life upon his release. He was employed as a consultant on the 1909 film of the Dalton gang's last stand, and wrote several books condemning criminality. He died in 1937.

Robert Clay Allison 'The Shootist'
1840-1887

Robert Clay Allison was no gentleman gunfighter. He was a moody and vicious man who bred fear in all who knew him. He was born in Tennessee, and joined the Confederate Army at the beginning of the Civil War. But he was soon discharged due to 'personality problems.' His discharge papers described him as 'incapable of performing the duties of a soldier because of a blow received many years ago. Emotional of physical excitement produces paroxysmals [sic.] of a mixed character, partly epileptic and partly maniacal.' Clay worked as a cattle hand after leaving the army, and moved to the Texan Brazos River Territory in 1865. He worked as a trail hand, driving cattle to New Mexico. Things obviously went well for him, as by 1870, he had acquired his own ranch in Colfax County, New Mexico. But local newspapers were already reporting that he had despatched as many as fifteen men, and he had a grim reputation for violence, especially when he was drunk.

His first truly notorious, and grotesque, killing happened in late 1870. Allison was drinking in a saloon when a hysterical woman approached him. She told him that her husband had gone mad and killed a number of his own ranch hands at their cabin, together with their own infant daughter. Allison rounded up a posse, but they found no bodies at the ranch. However, a few days later, bones were discovered on the property, and the ranch owner was arrested and imprisoned. Enraged by the man's behavior, Allison broke him out of jail, lynched him, and cut off his head, riding twenty-nine miles to Cimmaron with this gruesome trophy on a pole, before displaying the head in a local saloon. This kind of behavior did nothing to endear people to Allison, who was clearly mad. His presence also attracted other killers who wanted to enhance their own reputations by adding him to their list of kills. Chunk Colbert coolly invited Allison out to dinner before trying to shoot him under the table. Fortunately, Allison beat him to it, just as coffee was served. When he was asked why he had accepted a dinner invitation from a man he knew was out to kill him, Allison responded that he 'didn't want to send a man to hell on an empty stomach.'

His behavior became increasingly deranged. When a dental appointment to cure a raging toothache went awry, and the unfortunate dentist began to drill the wrong tooth, Allison furiously bundled him into his own chair and ripped off half the man's lip in trying to extract one of the dentist's own teeth.

Another event that demonstrates Allison's bizarre view of the world is the Bowie knife grave affair. He had fallen into dispute with a neighboring rancher, and suggested that they should settle their differences by digging a grave big enough to hold them both. They should then climb into the pit, each armed only with a Bowie knife, and see which one of them survived to climb out. The victor would arrange a tombstone for the vanquished. But events overtook Allison, and this encounter never took place. Driving supplies back from Pecos, Texas, he fell from the wagon, and one of the wheels ran over his neck, killing him instantly.

This rather ignominious end was unusual for a 'shootist' at this time. Men of this ilk generally expired in a hail of bullets, or dancing at the end of a rope.

Opposite page: Robert Clay Allison became increasingly deranged and was subject to violent mood swings and bizarre behavior. Here he is shown with his leg in plaster, having discharged his own gun before he drew. He died in a most unfortunate manner, being run over by his own wagon.

James Butler 'Wild Bill' Hickok
—— 1837-1876 ——

To this day, the reputation of Wild Bill Hickok epitomizes that of the gun fighting lawman; he was a 'genuine lover of law and order,' as well as a great showman and latter day duellist.

Hickok was born in Troy Grove, Illinois in 1837. He moved to Kansas in 1855, and was the town constable before reaching the age of 21. His career almost ended before it began when he inadvertently shot an unarmed man in his first killing. He was a contract scout, spy, and detective for the Union Army in the Civil War, and won the epithet 'Wild Bill' during this time. His reputation grew, and in 1871, the citizens of Abilene finally asked him to be their town marshal. Most of his predecessors in the job now lay in Boot Hill cemetery. They included the previous incumbent, pacifist Marshal Tom 'Bear River' Smith, who had been murdered by an axe-wielding homesteader. Not unreasonably, the weary citizens felt that a 'noted' and feared individual would stand a better chance of keeping the peace, particularly during the annual spring cattle drives. These generally resulted in the town being completely torn up by lawless cowboys. In fact, Hickok's reputation wasn't entirely deserved. He was a tremendous self-publicist who actively propagated the

Below: Hickok's
predecessor as town
marshal, Tom 'Bear River'
Smith was killed by an
axe-wielding home-
steader, and now resided
in Boot Hill cemetery.

fiction that he had killed over a hundred
white men – his tally was actually closer to
ten. He had worked as a scout during the
Civil and Indian Wars, and had been
elected sheriff of Hays County in 1869, but
it was his reputation for dealing with
frontier desperados that attracted Abilene.
Once installed as town Marshal, he
proceeded to clean up the town, running
Abilene from a card table in the Long
Branch Saloon, and earning a massive
$150 a month for his services. One
cowboy described him as looking like
a 'mad old bull' and he made every
attempt to look as intimidating as
possible. L'Amour describes his
habitual costume 'black frock coat, a
low-brimmed black hat, and two ivory-
butted and silver-mounted pistols thrust
behind a red silk sash.' In fact, the pistol
handles were worn reversed to speed his
draw. Hickok's larger-than-life presence
kept a lid on much of the town violence.

He was also surprisingly successful in
bringing gun control to the town,
disarming even reluctant Texans. He
posted a notice that disarmament would
be vigorously enforced, and the *Abilene
Chronicle* reported this. Their editorial
comment ran: 'There's no bravery in a
carrying revolvers in a civilized community.
Such a practice is well enough and
perhaps necessary when among Indians or
other barbarians, but among white people
it ought to be discountenanced.' Hickok's
poster is reminiscent of Matt Coburn's
'NOTICE' in Confusion,

*'To Thieves, Murderers,
and Short-card Artists
You are no longer welcome
in Confusion.
Those listed below can get out
or shoot it out,
And start any time they are ready.'*

As Marshal, Hickok was also responsible
for street cleaning, and kept the town
roads clear of dead dogs and horses. He
was also paid 50 cents for every stray dog

he shot. On one occasion, he was called
upon to despatch a mad Texas longhorn
that was rampaging through the town.
Hickok greatly enjoyed his time in
Abilene, rooming with a succession of
prostitutes, gambling, and drinking
heavily. The famous painter, N.C. Wyeth
painted a wonderfully atmospheric
portrait of a dandified Hickok unmasking
a card cheat in typical form. But his
tenure in the cow town came to a
disastrous end, when his deputy, Mike

Below: Jack McCall murdered the half-blind Bill Hickok
on August 2, 1876, to general public revulsion.
Hickok's tombstone bears Charley Utter's moving
epitaph, together with his incorrectly spelled name.

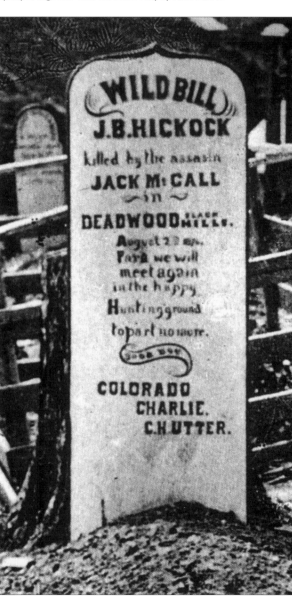

Williams, was killed in cross fire during a gunfight between Hickok and gambler Phil Coe. Hickok was devastated by Williams's death, weeping copiously as he laid his body on a snooker table in the Saloon. He paid for the deputy's funeral. After eight months of Hickok's 'cleanup,'

Abilene town council decided not to renew his expensive contract, and banned the cattle drives instead.

Jobless, Hickok drifted East, touring in a melodrama staged by Buffalo Bill, 'The Scouts of the Plains.' But he was hopeless in his starring role. By this time,

Above: Wild Bill was known for his dandified appearance.

War. When this violent feud finally wound up, The Kid's involvement on the side of the Regulators (who had been responsible for at least two murders) led to a life outside the law again. He was once more unable to find lawful employment, so he drifted about, gambling and cattle rustling. Knowing that the new Governor of the territory, Lew Wallace, wanted to re-establish order in Lincoln, The Kid turned himself in, offering to turn states evidence against other participants in the hostilities, an offer which was accepted by Governor Wallace. But when he realized that the court was loaded against him, Billy decided to escape once more.

By now, he was a celebrity, and his activities were widely reported in the newspapers, who coined the soubriquet 'Billy The Kid.' The Kid was reputedly fed up with having every murder in the West attributed to him, but admitted that 'I don't know, as anyone would believe anything good of me.' He managed to avoid capture for two years, but when he was framed for the murder of deputy James Carlyle, Pat Garrett was charged with bringing him in. Garrett finally caught up with The Kid on December 23, 1880, in a cabin in Stinkpot Springs. After a brief standoff, Billy surrendered. He was charged and sentenced for the murder of Sheriff Brady during the Lincoln County War, and was taken back to Lincoln to await his hanging. The Kid was fully aware that there could now be no reprieve so he made his final escape, killing guard J.W. Bell and taking time out to gun down Robert Olinger, who had bated him during his prison stay, with his own shotgun. The Kid reckoned that he wouldn't have shot Bell, except for the fact that he tried to run, but offered no apology for Olinger's despatch.

Public opinion now swung against the Kid, and Pat Garrett was charged, once again, with bringing him to justice. It took him three months to catch up with Billy in Fort Summer. A the very moment that Garrett was pumping rooming house owner Pete Maxwell for intelligence about the Kid's movements, Billy walked in to get a steak for dinner. Garrett felled the youngster with two bullets from his .45 caliber, single-action Colt, one of which lodged in his heart. The Kid spoke fluent Spanish, and his rather pathetic final words were 'Quien es? Quien es?' – 'Who is it?' 'Who is it?'

> *I'll sing you a true song of Billy the Kid*
> *I'll sing of the desperate deeds that he did*
> *Way out in New Mexico long, long ago*
> *When a man's only chance was*
> *his own forty four.*
>
> *When Billy the Kid was a very young lad*
> *In the old Silver City he went to the bad*
> *Way out in the West with a gun*
> *in his hand*
> *At the age of twelve years he first*
> *killed his man*
>
> *Now this is how Billy the Kid met his fate*
> *The bright moon was shining,*
> *the hour was late*
> *Shot down by Pat Garrett,*
> *who once was his friend,*
> *The young outlaw's life had now*
> *come to its end.*

> *Fair Mexican maidens play guitars*
> *and sing*
> *A song about Billy, their boy*
> *bandit king*

Billy's brief but colorful career as a gunman and outlaw was over. He was reputed to have gambled with Doc Holliday, dined with Jesse James, and gone target shooting with Bat Masterson. But

his advice to those that would follow in his footsteps was 'Advise persons never to engage in killing.' Many of his friends and acquaintances mourned his passing very sincerely, praising his sense of humor, loyalty to his friends, extreme bravery, and kindness to his horses. He looks a little simple in his portrait, but others spoke of his intelligence and cunning. Many also spoke derisively of Pat Garrett's self-interest. He gained the office of sheriff of Lincoln County for his work in killing The

Kid, and wrote the best-selling biography, THE AUTHENTIC LIFE OF BILLY THE KID: The noted Desperado of the Southwest.

Billy was certainly no 'good bad man.' By the time of his death, he was pretty well bad through and through, and many believed he was a cold-hearted murderer. But the teenage outlaw of the Southwest has left probably the biggest legend of any gun-slinging wrongdoer of the West, fueling a huge tourist industry in New Mexico.

Above: Billy the Kid looks slightly simple in this contemporary photograph, but must have had a certain charisma to generate such a massive personality cult.

Colt Frontier

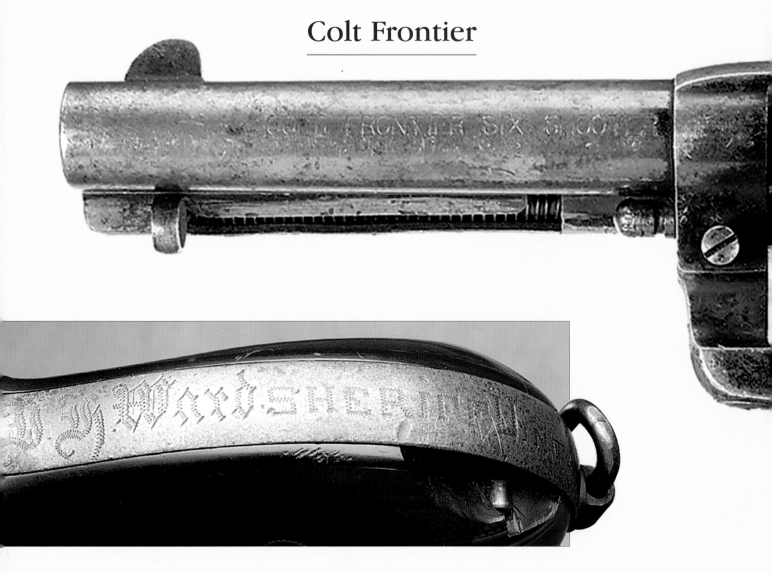

Above: The owners name, J. H. Ward, is emblazoned on the backstrap. Ward was the Sheriff of Vinta, Colorado.

Louis L'Amour liked to interject interesting guns into his plots. When we meet the mysterious stranger, Jonas, in opening chapter of THE MAN CALLED NOON, J.B. Rimes tosses him a gun, 'The gun was new, a Frontier model, and the weight of it on his hip was comforting.' Jonas appears to be suffering from memory loss caused by a bullet wound to the head. But Rimes can tell that he is used to bearing a weapon from the deft way that he catches the gun, checks it, and holsters it instinctively. This is the modus operandi of a gunfighter.

The 'Frontier model' in question is a Colt Frontier; the company launched the model in 1878. Popular calibers were .44-40 and .45 inch, with the barrel available in various lengths. Shorter barrels were more easily concealed and therefore of interest to plainclothes lawmen and criminals alike. The gun was a double

SPECIFICATIONS

Caliber: 0.44-40 inch

Length of barrel: 4 inches

Barrel shape: Round

Finish: Blue/gray mixed with surface rust

Grips: Hard Rubber

Action: Double

Year of manufacture: 1878

Manufacturer: Colt

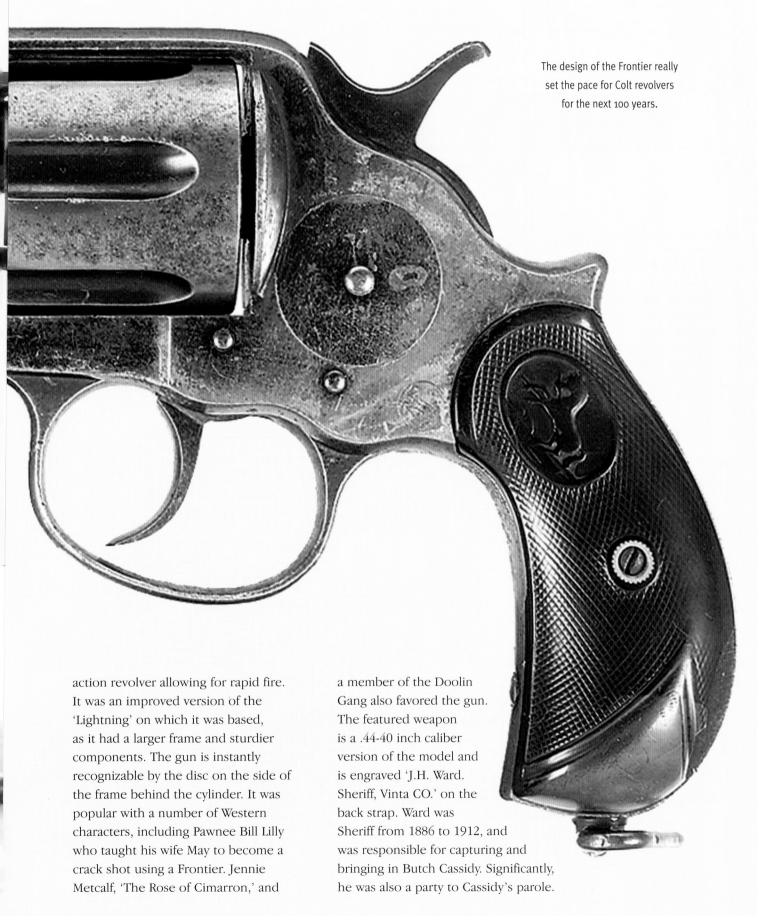

The design of the Frontier really set the pace for Colt revolvers for the next 100 years.

action revolver allowing for rapid fire. It was an improved version of the 'Lightning' on which it was based, as it had a larger frame and sturdier components. The gun is instantly recognizable by the disc on the side of the frame behind the cylinder. It was popular with a number of Western characters, including Pawnee Bill Lilly who taught his wife May to become a crack shot using a Frontier. Jennie Metcalf, 'The Rose of Cimarron,' and a member of the Doolin Gang also favored the gun. The featured weapon is a .44-40 inch caliber version of the model and is engraved 'J.H. Ward. Sheriff, Vinta CO.' on the back strap. Ward was Sheriff from 1886 to 1912, and was responsible for capturing and bringing in Butch Cassidy. Significantly, he was also a party to Cassidy's parole.

The Mormons

Opposite Page: A romantic depiction of the Mormon 'Saints' crossing the Mississippi around 1846, on the first stage of their journey West.

Below: The first waves of Mormon pioneers entering the Great Salt Lake Valley.

Louis L'Amour quite often refers to Mormons in his stories. Like so many other Westerners, they made the trek West for the sake of freedom, and in their case, to escape religious persecution. The first group of 'Saints' had crossed the Mississippi River in February 1846, on the first stage of the 'exodus' West. Brigham Young, who had read Fremont's description of the Valley of the Great Salt Lake, inspired their 1,400-mile long trek, and its destination. This trek would dominate the Church's history for the rest of the century. At first, the Mormons used covered wagons, then handcarts when their dray animals froze to death. But the journey to their final settlement in Utah was long and extremely hazardous and many pioneers died en route – seven

hundred in the first year alone. Once they reached their 'New Zion' in Utah, the Mormons imposed their civic order on the wild landscape in a very Eastern style, with wide streets and substantial buildings in stone, brick, and wood. They also established other Mormon colonies throughout a substantial swathe of the West, in Utah, Arizona, Nevada, and Idaho.

Many American literary figures have held a low opinion of Mormons. Mark Twain openly despised them (though he was forced to describe Salt Lake City as having 'a general air of neatness, repair, thrift and comfort'), and early Western writer Zane Grey often used them as his 'villains.'

But Louis L'Amour demonstrates a far higher regard for the sect, and so do his

characters. Utah Blaine advises Mary Blake to take refuge in the nearby Mormon settlement, obviously believing them to be decent and reliable. Borden Chantry reinforces this view. When he and Tyrel Sackett wonder if Mormon's could be involved in the recent spate of hold-ups (strangely, Utah has been spared), he discounts the theory, saying 'Most Mormons I've known were law-abiding folks.' Indeed, they are far more likely to be the victims of crime. Some of Ben Curry's gang have to be restrained from raiding their well-stocked farms.

Indeed, Mormons made a good living from helping other Westerners on their

way, especially the forty-niners. For some L'Amour characters, such as Mike Bastian, Salt Lake City is their only taste of civilization. Bastian also expresses admiration of their excellent tracking abilities. Mountain man Linus Rawlings has also visited 'Deseret,' saying that the Salt Lake was the most water he has ever seen.

Opposite page, top: A typical Mormon wagon train crossing the prairie.
Left: Many Mormons perished on their way West, in the harsh winter of 1856.

Above: An early view of Salt Lake City.
Top: The Mormons established way stations, such as Cove Fort, to provide shelter for early pioneers heading West.

Winchester 1866 Carbine

Right: The 1866 Carbine was named the 'Yellow Boy' after its distinctive brass receiver.

Throughout the L'Amour novels we find ourselves in the company of cowpunchers. This tough and individualistic breed grew up to service the big herds that were driven north from Texas in the years after the Civil War. The cattle were originally raised to feed the growing population of the West. But after the War, the majority were transported East via a growing railroad network. A transcontinental route was completed in

Above: The familiar slot in the side which received bullets. Normal loading was by thumbing the shells in.

1869, and a whole rail system was built in the following decade. A hungry East Coast market was waiting for Texan beef.

The Cowboy had very particular needs when it came to his choice of weapon and the Winchester Carbine fit them pretty well. The gun was easily carried in the saddle scabbard.

SPECIFICATIONS

Caliber: 0.44 inch rim fire cartridge

Length of barrel: 20 inches

Barrel shape: Round

Finish: Blue Steel Barrel, brass frame and receiver

Grips: Walnut

Action: Under lever repeating with 14 shot magazine

Year of manufacture: 1866-91

Manufacturer: Winchester Repeating Arms Company, New Haven, Connecticut

Its compact 20-inch barrel, with no bolt action or any other encumbrance, made it swift to draw and just as easy to stow. It featured a saddle ring on the left side of the frame for extra security and front and rear swivels for carrying on a sling. The polished brass frame and receiver gave its nickname 'Yellow Boy.'

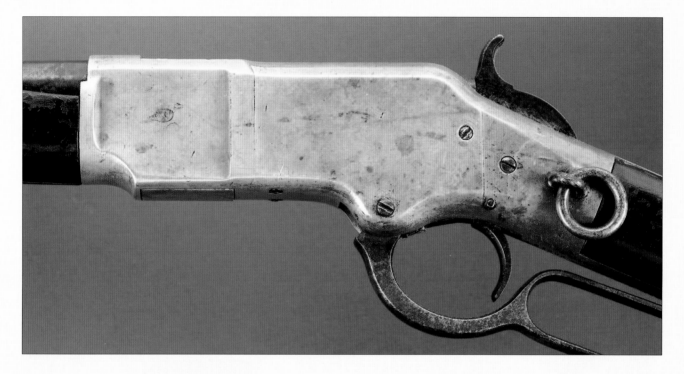

The .44-inch rim fire cartridge had its limitations when it came to ultimate power, but this was more than compensated for by its accuracy and ease of use. With fourteen shots and a quick reload action you could put two bullets into your intended target in the time that it took to aim a higher-powered single shot rifle. This was tremendously useful for a wide range of targets – game along the trail, a sick maverick, a gang of rustlers or a hunting party of Indians.

Indians also aspired to Winchester ownership, as it put them one step ahead of their adversaries in the United States Cavalry. For the most part, cavalrymen were still using Civil War issue, single shot weapons. Indians acquired the weapons either by capturing them from settlers, or from unscrupulous white traders. Indian versions were customized with brass and nickel-plated studs hammered in to the stock and fore grip, together with rawhide tassels and beadwork. Many examples have survived.

John Wayne also immortalized the weapon in the film TRUE GRIT. His version was modified with a loop under lever. In the film, Wayne demonstrates the technique of riding, firing, and reloading with one hand, and one eye! It is however debatable how many cowboys could afford this excellent gun because it was priced at a swingeing $40 – the exact monthly stipend of a 'forty-a-month cowhand.'

Above: Left side view shows carbine ring. At $40, cowhands weren't about to lose this gun.

Cowboys and Indians

Charles Goodnight
1836-1929

Oh, he would twirl that lariat and he didn't do it slow
He could catch them forefeet nine out of ten for any kind of dough
And when the herd stampeded he was always on the spot
And set them to milling, like the stirrings of a pot.

Right: Charles Goodnight, the greatest Western cowboy of them all. His story influenced many Louis L'Amour characters.

Nearly all L'Amour Western novels feature cowboys. He had a great respect for these men, and insisted that they were often intelligent romantics attracted to the perceived freedom of life on the Western trails. The term originally derived from the Spanish 'vaqueros,' and their equipment, clothing, and techniques of cattle management were greatly influenced by this connection. Although L'Amour accurately portrays the hard

Above: A cowboy attempts to round up the cattle, mouth covered against the dust.

lives of his 'forty-a-month-cowhand(s),' forced to work themselves 'half dead with tiredness,' he also credits them with a great deal of dignity, resourcefulness, and 'cow savvy.'

I've circled, herded, and night-herded too
But to keep you together is what I can't do
My horse is leg weary, and I'm awful tired
But if you get away I am sure to get fired
Bunch up, little doggies, bunch up.

L'Amour's father was involved in the cattle industry at one time, working as a state livestock inspector for the railroad in the family hometown, Jamestown. This was a hub of the Northern Pacific route.

Louis and his brothers encountered many cowboys in this way, travelling West, back to their ranches in North Dakota, or travelling East with stockcars full of cattle.

The greatest Western cowboy of them all was undoubtedly Charles Goodnight, the pioneer cattle king, whose larger-than-life story inspired L'Amour's cowpoke heroes. Goodnight's real-life fame spread throughout the West and inspired hundreds of men to try their luck in cattle ranching.

Charles Goodnight was born in Illinois in 1836, but his father decided to trek his family West in 1846 – The Year of Decision. The young Charles was obliged to ride bareback for seven hundred miles, as his family couldn't afford a saddle for

Above: A romantic evocation of the tough outdoor life of the cowboy.

Left: The life was tough, but the setting was truly magnificent.

Right and below right: Fine Western Saddles. Top is a Powder River Saddle made by the Denver Dry Goods Company. The blankets are Mexican and Navajo. Bottom has tooled leather with four plated tie down conchos on both sides and matching girth rings.

Below: Pair of tooled leather saddlebags. What few possessions the cowboy owned were consigned to them.

him.
He and his stepbrother quickly grew up to become cowhands, and as they were paid in calves, soon built up a small herd of some 180 head of cattle. But the outbreak of the Civil War virtually wiped them out. Charles became a Texas Ranger in 1857, fighting and scouting for the Confederacy in the Texas Panhandle. Years later, he described his situation, and that of the entire Texas cattle industry, when the hostilities were over, 'I suffered great

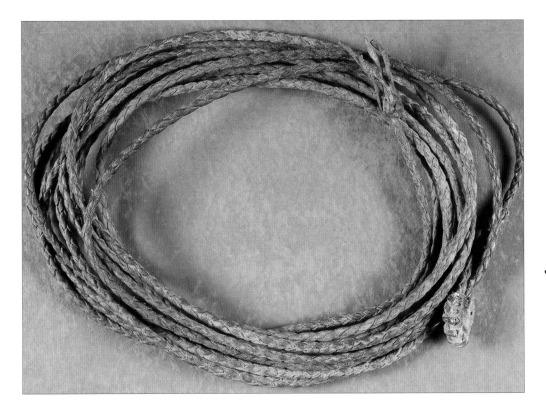

losses. The Confederate authorities had taken many of them (his cattle) without paying a cent. Indians had raided our herds and cattle thieves were branding them, to their own benefit without regard to our rights.' He joined in the Texas-wide roundup of stray cattle that became known as 'making the gather.'

Goodnight realized that he needed a business partner, and hitched up with Oliver Loving. Twenty-five years older than Charles, Loving was an experienced cattleman who had driven Texas longhorns all the way to Chicago.

Looking for a good business opportunity, the partners decided to drive their herd around the Comanche-infested Texas Panhandle to supply government agents in New Mexico. These agents were charged with feeding 8,000 reservation-bound Navajo, who were virtually starving for the lack of meat. It was 1866 when they set out on this very risky escapade. To avoid the threat of Indian attack, they took the longer, completely arid route through the 'the most desolate country.' Three hundred cattle died in the heat and a

Above: Goodnight's chuck wagon was the epicenter of life on the range.

hundred more thirst-crazed beasts drowned in a stampede at the Pecos River when they finally got there. Goodnight and Loving sold half the surviving herd to the reservation agents, and then continued on into Colorado, selling the remaining animals in Denver. The whole escapade netted the partners the huge sum of $24,000.

Not only did the pair forge the Goodnight-Loving trail, which became one of the most heavily used in the

drawers and compartments that contained the staples of the trail diet – flour, beans, coffee, pork, and canned tomatoes. The chuck wagon became the most critical piece of equipment used on

Below: Vital equipment for the trail.

the trail drives for decades, and a modern form remains in use on the larger ranches of today. L'Amour often refers to the chuck wagon – food (and especially hot coffee) was obviously hugely important to sustain the grindingly hard work of the trail. L'Amour's cowhands even describe themselves as 'riding the grub line,' and Barney Pike remembers how he would 'crawl out of bed on a chilly morning… (and) stagger half blind to the chuck wagon.' Barney even suggests that Eddie should put his cooking skills to good use as a trail cook. In fact, these men were quite well paid. Good food was highly prized by the trail bosses, as it could stop cowboys defecting to other outfits.

Goodnight also worked to perfect a unique method of driving cattle. He put the trail boss out in front, the horse herd and chuck wagon behind him, followed in turn by the point riders and lead steers, with the bulk of the herd coming next, kept together by flank riders, with drag riders coming up the rear, preventing stragglers from falling behind.

Loving decided that the next step should be for him and Goodnight to win government beef contracts at Bosque

Southwest, but Goodnight also invented and constructed the first chuck wagon, drawn by oxen. The wagon was equipped with a chuckbox, whose hinged lid dropped down to become a cook's worktable. Inside the box were various

Above: Duster Wyman wears Levis in HANGING WOMAN CREEK.

Right: Jangling spurs were music to a cowboy's ears.

Below right: John Batterson was the inventor of the Stetson, originally known as the 'Boss of the Plains.'

Below: Hide gloves were practical and rather dandyish.

Redondo. Unfortunately, the Comanche caught up with Loving on the open plain, wounding his wrist and side. Despite being rescued, gangrene set into the wounds, and Loving died as Goodnight reached his bedside. Goodnight described him a 'one of the coolest and bravest men I have ever known, but devoid of caution.' Grief-stricken, he constructed a special casket from discarded tin cans to carry the body of his friend back to Texas, to honor his dying wish.

L'Amour shows several examples of this close emotional bond between male 'partners' working the trails. Perhaps Barney Pike and Eddie Holt are his supreme example of this kind of relationship, which vastly increased the likelihood of survival for both men. They play to each other's strengths and watch each other's backs. They even seem to have a rather cosy domestic life together; Barney greatly appreciates Eddie's good

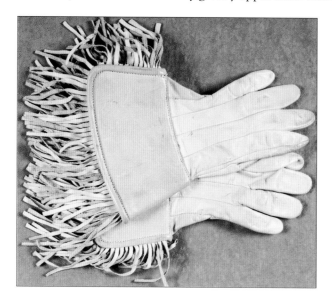

home cooking.

Goodnight married Mary Ann Dyer in 1869, and like many L'Amour heroes – including Utah Blaine – decided to settle down at this point in his life. As he said 'After I married I thought I would no longer follow my wild trail life. I concluded to settle down and take up ranching instead.' He duly bought land in

Colorado, but like many L'Amour characters, he missed the freedom of the trail, the excitement, coffee from the chuck wagon… sourdough biscuits.

Goodnight took the opportunity of running his own spread to learn a good deal about land management. Overgrazing was a serious hazard of ranching, and Barney Pike, L'Amour's archetypal cowhand, discusses how different types of grass stand up to this. 'Blue gama… mixed with buffalo grass. It'll stand a lot of grazing, and it re-seeds itself.' Goodnight also pioneered work in cattle breeding; crossbreeding the tough Texas longhorn with Herefords to achieve financially lucrative animals. He also interbred buffalos with domestic cattle to produce 'cattalos.' Like many of his class, he was also active in enforcing vigilante justice against cattle rustlers and horse thieves.

But, for the second time in his life, Goodnight was financially wiped out in the 'Panic' of 1873. He found that all he had left to his name were 1800 longhorns. Never one to give in, he formed a business partnership with Irishman John G. Adair, who backed him to set up the JA Ranch, the first in the Comanche-Kiowa buffalo land. By this time, the Comanches had all but given up the struggle, and Goodnight felt it was safe to move back to the Panhandle. Goodnight established the new ranch in the legendary Palo Duro Canyon, where an abundant supply of sweet, fresh water meant that the grass was always green. The importance of this find could not be overestimated. As L'Amour says 'to the cattlemen water and grass were their very life blood.'

The partnership between Goodnight and Adair lasted for eleven years. By the time Goodnight decided he wanted to have his own land again; they had built up a herd of 100,000 head of cattle grazing a one million acre ranch. Goodnight described how 'to care for them (the cattle) over such an extensive range we employed a little army of men called 'cowboys'.' For the first time, the word had come into general usage. Goodnight had a very paternal relationship with these men, forbidding them to drink, gamble, swear, or even play cards in the bunkhouse. Unfortunately, this meant that when they

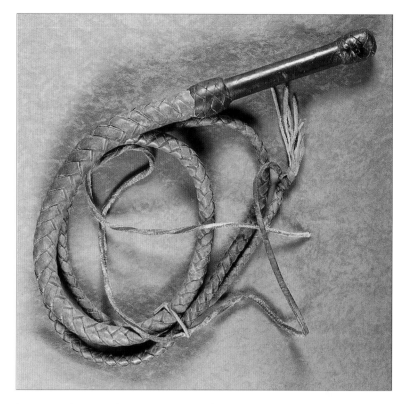

hit town, his 'cowboys' were completely out of control, and developed a dismal reputation.

Goodnight made a cool half million dollars from his venture with Adair. Just like Tom Gatty in HANGING WOMAN CREEK, he had started off as a

Above: A trail manager's whip.

Below: A cowboy's best friend was his horse.

become more profitable. Barney Pike explains how trail bosses rode the trains to explore new pasture, and to get ahead of migrating herds. Finished cattle were shipped on the hoof from railhead towns like Abilene (America's first cow town, where Illinois businessman J.C. McCoy built his cattle market in 1867), Ellsworth, and 'Jimtown' (Jamestown). The stock was then railed to Eastern hubs such as Chicago, St. Louis, and Rock Island. By the 1880s, the advent of refrigeration cars meant that Western beef could be transported all the way to Europe. Barney and Eddie also ride the Iron Horse, carrying their saddles, looking for their next cowhand jobs.

It was at this, Goodnight's last ranch, where the inveterate plainsman died at the age of 93, having survived for years on a trail diet of coffee, beef, and Cuban cigars.

Goodnight was not only the father of the Western cowboy, but he had lived their legend to the fullest. He was the first and last of the great frontier cattlemen.

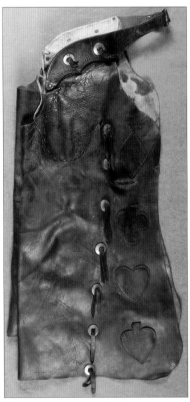

Above: A pair of buffalo chaps. Eddy wears a pair that he has from his days in a Wild West show.

cowpuncher, and ended up a rich and powerful man through herding cattle. He now established a ranch on land along the route of the Fort Worth and Denver City Railroad. A town bearing his name duly sprang up. The cattle business had used the railroad from its earliest introduction into the West. By this time, cattle ranching rivalled mining as the dominant industry of the region, and exploited every possible advance to

Above: A romantic view of cowboy life.

Left: Goodnight and Adair built up a herd of 100,000 cattle.

Below: Cattle being driven into stock pens at a rail head.

Henry Rifle

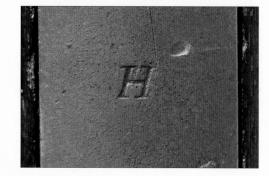

Left: 'H' for Henry is stamped on all the major components.

SPECIFICATIONS

Caliber: 0.44 inch

Length of barrel: 24 inches

Barrel shape: octagonal

Finish: Brown patina

Grips: Walnut

Action: Lever Action 15 shot repeater

Year of manufacture: 1864

Manufacturer: New Haven Arms Company, New Haven, Connecticut

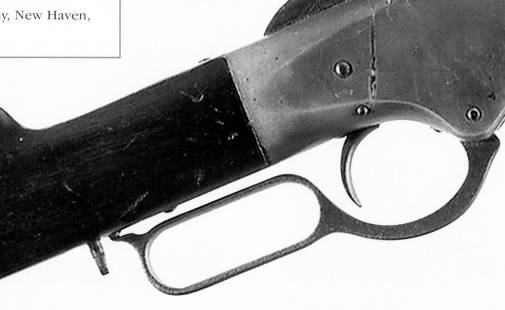

Oliver Winchester appointed Benjamin Tyler Henry as plant superintendent at the New Haven Arms Company in 1858. One of his key tasks was to develop reliable cartridges for the failed Volcanic lever action rifle. The result was not only improved cartridges, but also a completely new gun design patented by Henry on October 16, 1860. This new rifle was a 15 shot repeater with lever action, which used a .44 rim-fire copper cartridge. This fired a round-nosed, grooved lead bullet propelled by 26-28 grains of black powder. Muzzle velocity was 1200 feet per second, a huge improvement over the 700 fps of the Volcanic. The gun had a standard 24 inch barrel, apart from a few experimental

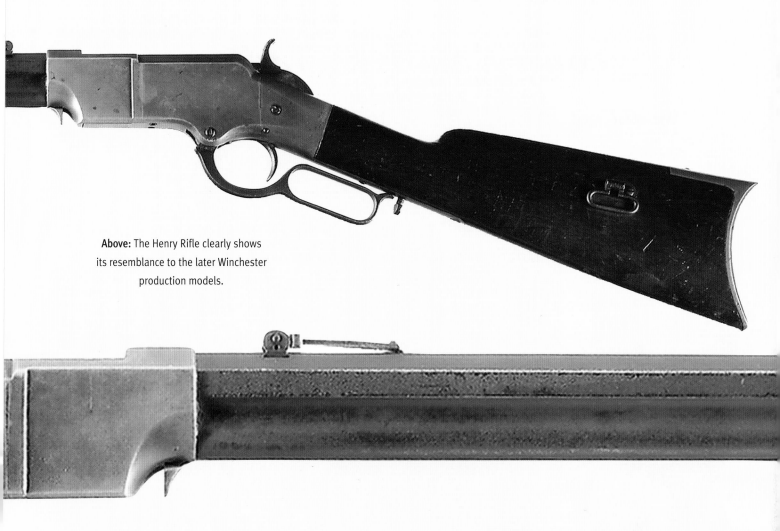

Above: The Henry Rifle clearly shows its resemblance to the later Winchester production models.

models, which had shortened barrels. This latter innovation was an attempt to reduce the 9 pound weight of the weapon. The frame was made from either iron or brass.

In six years of production, 14,000 examples were manufactured, including 1,731 purchased by the army at the end of the Civil War.

The Henry is the rifle of choice in L'Amour's OVER ON THE DRY SIDE (1975). Both Doby Kernohan, a young settler and the novel's hero Owen Chantry, use them. Doby reflects, 'I never had but just the rifle. I'd always wanted me one of them pistols, but we never had the money for it. I had me a rifle and a good one too – a Henry. I also carried a Bowie a man could shave with, it was that sharp.' So the Henry is seen as a standard

element of western gear, just like the Bowie knife. This was the kind of equipment that kept frontier men alive.

Our featured weapon bears a relatively high serial number and is believed to have been part of the military issue and to troops on guard duty in Washington D.C. towards the end of the war. Many of these guns then found their way back into the civilian hands of frontiers people when the War was over. It has a polished brass frame, and is stamped 'H' for Henry on the lower tang. Unlike the later 1866 Winchester, the magazine is loaded from the front of the tube under the barrel, and not through the familiar loading gate on the right side of the frame. Nelson King developed the side-loading system. He was later a plant superintendent.

Above: The brass frame is noticeably devoid of the side receiver slot and the heavy octagonal barrel – both features that identify this as a Henry.

Above: Arikara warrior Bear's Belly, clad in a grizzly bear hide. They were close cousins of the Pawnee and very warlike.

reflected the conditions of the territory they occupied. The region was vast, and the climate varied hugely from the icy north to the sweltering south. As Zeb Rawlings says in HOW THE WEST WAS WON, 'before the coming of the white man, (the Indian) had adapted himself to his surroundings to a remarkable degree.'

The Plains, or red, Indian is perhaps the closest to the recognizable cliché of Western films, complete with impressive war bonnet and pony. In reality, the people of the Plains were semi-nomadic and non-agricultural, living mainly in semi-permanent villages on the edge of the plain lands. The main tribes of this area were the Assinboine, Arapaho, Kiowa, Kiowa-Apache, Sarsi, and Teton-

Dakato. All of these tribes were completely dependent on the buffalo for their clothing, tepees, cooking utensils, tools, and weapons and lived on a diet that consisted, almost exclusively, of buffalo meat. They had originally hunted on foot, but their lives were revolutionized when white men introduced the horse to America. Plains Indians had no wheels, but had developed the 'travois' method of hauling meat and supplies. This was a tough sheet of rawhide mounted on two poles, first pulled by dogs, then horses.

The Rocky Mountain plateau region was mainly settled by the Flathead, Kutenai, Nez Perce (who later helped Lewis and Clark and their way West), Paiute, Ute, and Yakima tribes. Some of these Native Americans were hunters; others were hunter-gatherers. Other tribes looked down on the latter, derisively terming them 'diggers.'

The Pueblo Indians of the Southwest were more successful, developing all kinds of intricate crafts such as pottery, cotton weaving, and turquoise jewelery-making. They had sophisticated religious rituals,

Above: A war dance.

Below: The stone houses of the Pueblo people, whose descendents still live in the Southwest.

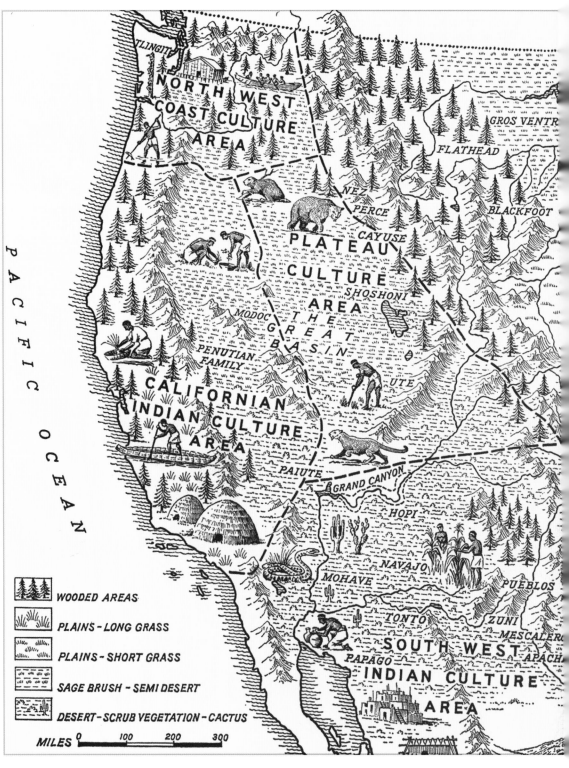

Above: A Cheyenne warrior with war bonnet beautifully crafted with ermine drops and beaded brow band. His sash is also beaded with a star motif.

lived in stone houses, and traded with tribes in Mexico. But the Pueblos ultimately fell victim to the other tribes of the region – the warlike Navahos and Apaches, who lived from raiding and hunting.

The benign Californian climate meant that Indians from this region (such as the Modoc and Penutian Family) were able to retain a very simple existence. They only wore clothes in the winter, and lived off a diet of acorn flour. They also constructed primitive balsa rafts of bundled rushes, but their only claim to dexterity was their refined basket weaving.

By complete contrast, the Tlingit people of the Northwest had such an

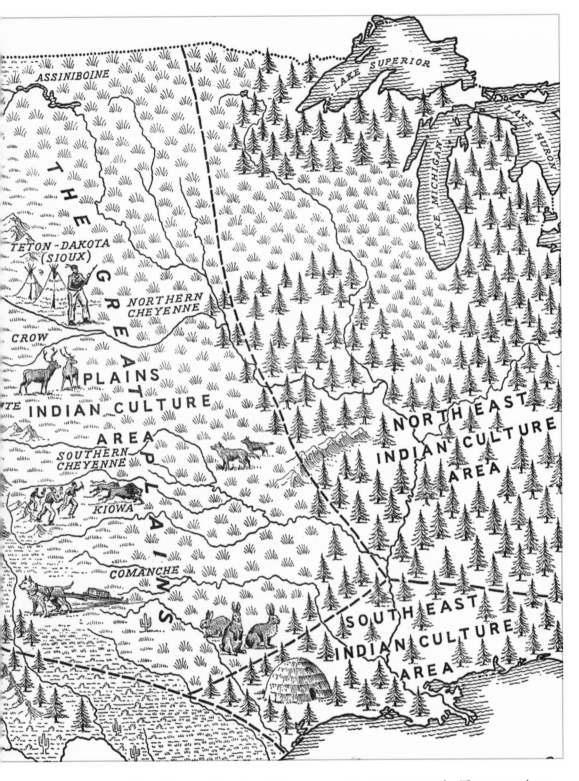

Left: A map showing the distribution of the Native American tribes at the time of the expansion West.

Below: Yellow Shirt, a Sioux warrior, holding the sacred Horse Dance stick in his right hand and a beaded pipe and tobacco bag in his left.

abundance of food (especially salmon) in the rivers and the ocean, and a profusion of cedar wood, that they were able to construct a very sophisticated society. They lived in elaborate wooden halls up to five hundred feet long, held 'potlachs' (ritual feasts), celebrated complex religious ceremonies, and each family carved itself an intricate totem pole. They were also a sea-going people, building fabulous cedar canoes that held up to fifty people.

But the Mexican Aztecs were the most advanced Indian society that the white invaders came upon. The Aztecs had conquered the original Mayan and Toltec peoples to establish a quasi-military state

Below: Hudson's Bay Indian Trade Musket, made by Hollis & Sons.

Right: a beautiful pair of beaded soft hide moccasins. Mountain men also adopted these.

Below: The 'travois' was used to haul meat and supplies. It was originally pulled by dogs.

in the fourteenth century, and had developed wonderful crafting abilities. In many ways, it is clear that Louis L'Amour and several of his heroic characters view the Indians and their tribal knowledge as the key to the new world. In TO THE FAR BLUE MOUNTAINS, Barney Sackett acknowledges that he will 'learn much from them about this country.' He accurately describes their simple way of life, 'mostly hunting and gathering berries, roots and nuts, they need much land to support only a few… some of the tribes… plant corn… (but) mostly they live by hunting, fishing, and gathering, so they move from time to time, going to new areas where they can find more game, and more food.' Although his party suffers from Indian attack, Indians also help the Sacketts to survive their first winter in the New World, teaching them how to make buckskin clothes and moccasins, and how to live off the land.

L'Amour uses Barney Sackett's experience to illustrate his unsentimental view of the Indian. On the one hand, Barney has an Indian friend – the Eno, Potaka – and rescues Wa-ga-su from the brutal Tuscarora. He instructs his men to treat Indians as their equals, and their women with respect. But he meets his end at the hands of a Seneca, who sings him a ceremonial death-song. Despite this, there is a feeling of mutual regard and honor, even in death. The old chief asks 'Who now is left to test our young braves?'

Indian stories, legends, and history are a thread woven throughout L'Amour's books. There are numerous examples of

how true plainsmen have espoused Indian ingenuity, to work with, rather than against, the land. Utah Blaine makes a pot out of bark, an 'Injun trick,' to boil water to tend the dying Kelsey's wounds, and grinds a maize poultice for Timm's wounds. 'This was, he recalled, and Indian remedy that he had seen used long ago.' Later, he collects 'a stack of herbs used by the Indians to doctor wounds.'

Tracking, a highly valued plainsmen ability ('To a

Western plainsman, a track was as easily read as a road sign') is also recognized as an Indian skill. Utah Blaine is so able a tracker that he is described as 'an Injun on the trail,' while Mike Bastien (SON OF A WANTED MAN) can 'track like an Apache.' Indeed, Bastien wears Indian moccasins for tracking work, getting as close as possible to nature, 'skilled in the arts of the wilds.' Linus Rawlings, another L'Amour

character who is deeply in touch with nature, 'had great respect for the Indian. He knew him, not as a poor heathen of whom the white man took advantage, but as a fierce fighting man who lived for war and Horse-stealing.' It is almost as though the Indians are seen as an organic element of the Western landscape itself, which was 'sacred to the Indians, (with) the great peaks they revered.'

Below: This beaded hide shirt demonstrates the exquisite artistry of the native peoples.

Below: Indians draw buffalo into a canyon to make for an easier kill.

Right: Blackfeet Indians set John Colter free, but nude, assuming that he wouldn't last for long in the desert. They were one of the most aggressive tribes, and were opposed to the mountain men defiling their lands.

To some extent, this view of the native plainspeople means that L'Amour is able to avoid dealing with any moral issue about white settlement. This he generally represents as a good thing, as taming the 'wild country.' In HOW THE WEST WAS WON, L'Amour unsentimentally catalogs how the tribes were 'forced to move West during the Indian removal.' But his hero

Zeb Rawlings, a soldier charged with protecting the railroad workers from Indian attack, has a surprisingly positive view of the Native Americans. 'Like many another soldier who served on the frontier…(he) had developed a sympathy for the Indian… he did not believe them a pack of savages to be killed off like so many mad dogs.' L'Amour takes this a degree further, equating bad treatment of the Indian with moral bankruptcy. Men who disregard the Indians, like railroad boss Mike King, are men of a lower caliber. He only values what he regards as the 'superior culture' and technical skill of the white man, 'I don't have any love for the noble red man, and never did.' Men like him have only come to the West to exploit it. King's greed and folly lead him to break his word, and push the 'blazing and iron trail for the Iron Horse' through the Arapahoe hunting grounds. This brings death and destruction down on his own people, including Zeb's uncle, tracklayer Sam Prescott.

Throughout the novels, the incursion of white settlers into the West is more or less opposed and repulsed by the native peoples. Zeb Rawlings' post-army career flounders when he loses half his cattle during a pitched battle with the Kiowa, who also drove Matt Coburn off his ranch. Roger Morgan's wagon train is attacked by Cheyenne. Arapahoe braves, with faces 'painted with streaks of black' attack the settlers' town, while 'a bad Indian, the Tonkawa Kid… killed and robbed a farming family.'

L'Amour carefully categorizes the degrees of antagonism displayed by the differing tribes. Some like the Shoshones and Flatheads can co-exist with the frontier people. The Nez Perce even boast that they have never killed a white man. Other groups, like the Sioux, Cheyenne, and Arapahoe are more opportunistic, while L'Amour describes the Ute, 'next to the Blackfeet no tribe was more trouble to the white man.' That is, if you discount the Seris, said to be cannibals, one of whom trails Catlow through 'meat hunger.' The Iroquois are also described as 'very savage,' and Catlow refers to the land of the Comanches, Apaches, Tonkawa, and Tamahumara as being full of 'wild animals and wilder Indians.'

L'Amour also describes the gradual integration of several tribes into the settled Western lands – a real-life phenomenon. He describes the 'Five civilized tribes – the Cherokees, Choctaws, Chickasaws, Creeks, and Seminoles. Most of them lived like white men. A good many had education, a good many were veterans of the war, and others had ancestors who had fought with or against Jackson.'

Above: Geronimo of the Apaches. Like many Indians, he seems curiously diminished by ordinary western clothing.

The Buffalo Hunters

Below: A Buffalo Hunter's kit believed to be the best preserved and most complete to have survived from the days of the Frontier.

From the early part of the nineteenth century, the Plains were gradually stripped of their herds of buffalo. Early pioneers like the mountain men killed them to provide food as a means of survival, as the Indians had done to supplement their diet, and to provide clothing and shelter.

However, these small inroads into the population of the herds were nothing compared to the wholesale slaughter that occurred following the Civil War.

Western expansion led to the view that everything was there to be exploited and as a result the mighty herds were hunted down and slaughtered to the gates of extinction. Many of the hides and meat was shipped back east to the ready markets but an increasing proportion went to sustain life in the growing frontier towns. To fulfill this need, a breed of professional hunters came into being – men who killed to sustain the 'market' for Buffalo products, and who killed coolly and scientifically with the modern weapons at their disposal in the latter half of the nineteenth century. In the early days of smoothbore flintlocks – the only weapons available in the early years of the century – killing game as large as a Buffalo required skill.

Below: Mountain men pursue the herd on horseback to get a close range shot.
Bottom: The herds are now re-established after virtual extinction.

A close shot was necessary to penetrate the animal's thick hide, which meant careful stalking.

As weapons technology developed – largely during the Civil War – more powerful breech loading rifles became available, which made mass slaughter of the herds a reality. Our spread (pages 122-123) shows a complete Market Buffalo Hunter's outfit which comprises a Sharps Model 1874 'Old Reliable' hunting rifle in its original Buffalo fur

covered travelling box. With it is a complete collection of butcher knives in fur covered wooden blocks, and also a cylindrical water canteen with a wire handle. Three photos survive with the collection: one of Buffalo skinners, a mounted Buffalo head, and a studio

portrait of the hunter's brother. It is believed from the excellent condition of this equipment that it would have been carefully transported on a wagon to the scene of the hunt and only then removed from the protective boxes in the immediate vicinity of the herd.

Western conservation in the twentieth century enabled the herds to be reintroduced and they can now be seen grazing in growing numbers *(bottom left)*, a scene which harks back to that witnessed by the first western explorers.

Above: Early hunters used every means at their disposal to hunt Buffalo. This group is setting fire to the prairie in order to stampede the herd toward a group of well armed trappers.

Spencer Sports or Buffalo Rifle

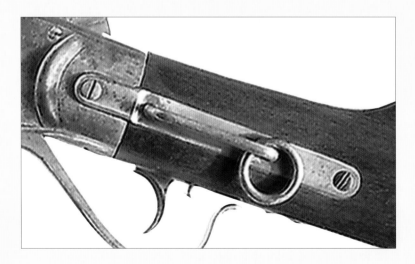

Below: The sliding carbine ring was a leftover from the original carbine version of the gun.

L'Amour features the Spencer in UTAH BLAINE. The grasping Nevers is intent on seizing Mary Blake's B-Bar Ranch, and rides out with twenty of his hands. In contrast, only three men, Rip Coker, Dan Timm, and the novel's hero, Utah Blaine, defend the B-Bar. Timm packs the Spencer. He is a trusted older hand, who was a friend to Mary's murdered father. During the nighttime standoff, Coker is armed with a Winchester rifle but he passes this off as the even more fearsome Colt Revolving Shotgun. But as L'Amour points out 'The Spencer .56 was no bargain either.' Timm stays out of sight, 'bedded down by the stone well in the

SPECIFICATIONS

Caliber: 0.45 inch

Length of barrel: 32 inches

Barrel shape: Octagonal

Finish: Brown

Grips: Walnut

Action: Single shot / breech loading

Year of manufacture: c1872

Manufacturer: A. J. Plate, San Francisco, California

vague light. "Yeah," Timm's voice came from the well coping. "You hombres make a right tempting target. This Spencer can't miss at this range!"' The combined firepower of the three men is enough for Nevers and his men to back off. 'Nevers found his voice. "All right," he said eventually, "We'll go. But by daylight we'll be back."'

In fact, the Spencer rifle was a fairly specialist weapon. It was based on the well-proven military version used by both sides in the Civil War. It could be

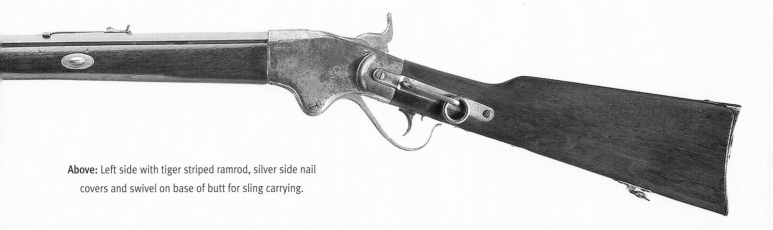

Above: Right side detail shows Civil War carbine action lock coupled with heavy duty octagonal barrel.

Above: Left side with tiger striped ramrod, silver side nail covers and swivel on base of butt for sling carrying.

employed as both a carbine and a rifle. The single shot breech loading action used a rim fire cartridge and was a great improvement, both in terms of speed of loading and handling, over the muzzle loading rifles that both sides started out with.

When adapted for Western use, the gun was equipped with a longer, heavier and usually octagonal barrel. This allowed for a larger caliber of up to .56 of an inch, and had the effect of reducing the kick on firing. These modifications greatly improved the gun's effectiveness at long range and its ability to stop a Buffalo – or a man – made it a good choice.

The famed Western gun dealer A. J. Plate of San Francisco rebuilt this particular example. Plate's name is stamped on the barrel.

Great Institutions of the West
The Texas Rangers:
Men Who could not be Stampeded

Right: In the absence of any real protection from the Mexican government, Austin ('The Father of Texas') recruited ten good men to protect the new territory. They became the nucleus of the Texas Rangers.

In Louis L'Amour's West, law enforcement ranges from judicial law upheld by appointed officers, right through to lynch mob justice. The closest thing to an official police force in the West (as opposed to individual lawmen) was the outfit known as the Texas Rangers. L'Amour mentions these elite men many times. His marshals and sheriffs have often served with the Rangers. Indeed, the Rangers' tracking and detective methods formed the blueprint for professional law enforcement on the frontier.

For example, in HOW THE WEST WAS WON, ex-army officer Zeb Rawlings serves two years in the Texas Rangers, following a disastrous stint ranching. He ends up as a deputy US marshal, operating in the Indian Territory. Zeb is the kind of lawman that Louis L'Amour admired, and it's significant that his post-army career in enforcement begins with the Rangers.

But the harshness of Western conditions, and the many temptations on offer meant that the barrier between the law officer and criminal was more permeable than it is today. Men crossed and re-crossed this divide in real life, and do so in L'Amour's novels. In CATLOW, L'Amour describes several Texas Rangers who have switched to the other side,

Opposite page: Remember the Alamo. The 'Last Stand' defense of this mission fort against overwhelming Mexican forces took place in 1836. This was the year in which Texas declared itself to be an independent republic. The defense of the Alamo became a patriotic symbol of American resistance to the domination of foreign powers.

becoming professional man hunters, putting their renowned tracking skills to work for personal gain. Hired gunmen and killers often started out with respectable backgrounds in the army and as officers of the law, just like Matt Giles who had 'begun his killing as a mere boy in the Moderators and Regulators wars of northeast Texas, and had graduated to a sharpshooter in the Confederate Army' before going irredeemably bad.

The origins of the Texas Rangers stretch back to the earliest days of Anglo settlement in Texas, and the organization is now the oldest law enforcement agency in North America with statewide jurisdiction. At the beginning of the nineteenth century, the territory of Texas was controlled by Mexico, and the Austins (father and son Moses and Stephen) were hired by the Mexican government to recruit settlers for the new land. But Mexico soon proved to be completely unable, or unwilling, to protect the new settlers from Indian attack. In 1823, Stephen Austin recruited a fledgling force of ten men 'to act as rangers for the common defense.' This was a positively revolutionary idea for the time, when Western law enforcement was at best patchy and informal.

This original force of 'ranging' officials is credited with being the forerunner of the contemporary Texas Rangers. They went on to become not only an effective force for law enforcement, but one of the most mythological elements in the history of the Old West, a focus of traditional values. They 'ranged' the length of the new colony, protecting the white settlers from attack by a whole roster of Indian tribes, including the Comanche, Karankawa, Waco, Tehuacani, and Tonkawa. When no threat was apparent, the men returned to their own land and families.

A Corps of professional, full-time Rangers was established a few years later, whose members were paid $1.25 a day (for 'pay, rations, clothing and horse service'). In this way, the men were responsible for providing their own arms, mounts and equipment and many Rangers carried examples of the newly introduced Colt revolving pistols, from the recently established company.

Before the involvement of the Austins, only a tiny number of colonists had made it to Texas by 1821 (an estimated 600-700). But despite attempts by the Mexican government to limit the number of settlers coming into Texas via the US, an estimated 50,000 Americans settled in the state between 1823 and 1836. Inevitably, this led to a schism of opposing interests opening up between the new American Texans and the Mexican government. This bad feeling led to the wrongful imprisonment of Stephen F. Austin for over two years in Mexico City (accused of 'inciting revolution' against the Mexican regime), when he tried and failed to negotiate improved rights for the white settlers. Not unnaturally, this experience converted Austin (the 'Father of Texas') from a moderate man willing to negotiate with Mexico to a fervent

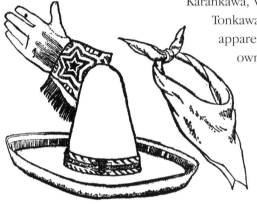

Above: The Rangers' costume owed more than a nod to traditional Mexican dress.

believer in the Texas Independence movement. He went on to become a volunteer commander in the Texas Revolution.

When a provisional 'rebel' government, (known as the Permanent Council) was established by the 'Consultation of 1835,' one of its first acts was to recruit twenty-five professional Rangers under the command of Silas M. Parker. Their primary duty was to 'range' the frontier between Brazos and the Trinity. This force grew to consist of three companies of 56 men, each commanded by a captain together with first and second lieutenants with a major in overall charge of the force.

In the heat of the Revolutionary war, men often served as both soldiers and Rangers. Some Rangers were drafted into cavalry regiments, and were known as dragoons. The Gonzales Ranging Company of Mounted Volunteers, for example, was the only fighting force to answer Colonel Travis's desperate plea for assistance in defending the mission fort of the Alamo (1836) from the overwhelming force of 5,000 Mexican troops. The Rangers died heroically alongside the other defenders, who included famous scout, hunter, and Indian fighter Davy Crockett.

'The Last Stand' became a potent symbol of American resistance to foreign domination and was instrumental in Texas joining the Union in 1845. Several other Rangers were captured by the Mexican commander, General Santa Anna, and were amongst the 350 people that he ordered to be slaughtered on Palm Sunday 1836, in fields just outside Goliad. This massacre, and that of the Alamo, became the focus of Texan revolutionary fervor, and the origin of Sam Houston's famous battle cry 'Remember the Alamo, Remember Goliad.'

The Tumlinson Rangers were also involved in the struggle, fighting a rearguard action to protect the shattered

Texan army as it retreated in the 'runaway scrape.' Other Rangers served as scouts for the Texan military forces, and won a tremendous reputation for their brilliant tracking skills. Individual Rangers, such as Jack Hays, Ben McCulloch, Samuel Walker, and 'Bigfoot' Wallace became famous as frontier fighters. They were also getting better equipped. In 1839, the Rangers became the first civilian force to be armed with Colts. The Texas Government bought 180 holster-sized pistols (these were saddle, rather than belt holsters) for their use. These weapons were five-shot, .36 caliber, nine-inch barrelled, revolving pistols of the type that Colt had first patented in 1835. Samuel Walker, a contemporary Ranger who rode for Captain Jack Hays, wrote to Samuel Colt in England, 'The pistols which you made… have been in use by the Rangers for three years… In the summer of 1844, Col. J. Hays with 15 men fought about 80

Camanche [sic] Indians, boldly attacking them on their own ground, killing and wounding about half their number… Without your pistols we would not have had the confidence to have undertaken such daring adventures.'

Ultimately, the Texan forces' policy of attrition won the day, and the current border between the two countries was established. But there were continual skirmishes along the Mexican side of the Rio Grande for the next ten years. In fact, Rangers were making punitive strikes into Mexico well into the twentieth century. In one battle of 1917, it is thought that the Rangers may have killed as many as twenty Mexicans. Despite this, Mexicans and Indians have both been counted amongst the ranks of the Rangers. As early as the 1830s, an Indian nicknamed 'Bravo Too Much' rode with the most famous early Ranger, John Coffee ('Jack') Hays.

Above: The Gonzales Ranging Company of Mounted Volunteers was the only fighting force to answer Colonel Travis's desperate pleas for assistance in defending the Alamo from over 5,000 Mexican troops. The Rangers died heroically alongside the other defenders.

Below: The Texas Rangers used the first Colt revolvers in their defense work. They effectively neutralized several Indian tribes with the weapon.

Once Texan independence had been achieved, the next step was to re-tame the colony – by establishing the rule of law, and repelling Indian attack. The Rangers proved to be a cost-effective way of achieving both of these aims. Their role became more inward looking, and although they had been known as 'los diablos Tejanos' (The Texas Devils) for their effectiveness against Mexican guerrillas, the responsibility for defending the international border gradually devolved upon the US army. In response to this, the number of Rangers began to dwindle.

The Texas Rangers also played an important role in the Civil War. Many enlisted in 'Terry's Texas Rangers' (commanded by the brilliant Colonel E. Terry) and were a great boost to the strength of the Confederate Army. Despite seceding in 1861, and for the duration of the Civil War, Texas was readmitted to the Union in 1870.

During the post war period of

reconstruction, the role of the Rangers was assumed by the highly political and widely disliked State Police, who were charged with the implementation of the deeply unpopular 'carpetbagger' laws. This resulted in the institution falling into disrepute amongst war-weary Texans. But following the repeal of the carpetbag rule in 1873, the service was reformed.

The Texas Legislature ordered the formation of two Ranger forces in 1874; the Frontier Battalion, led by Major John B. Jones and the Special Force, led by Captain Leander McNelly. At this time, an increased level of external security had led to a huge upsurge in internal lawlessness, so the Rangers developed a different role as law enforcers, while continuing their fight against insurgents. They effectively neutralized the formerly powerful Comanche and Kiowa, by fighting such famous skirmishes as the Battle of Plum Creek. But the new Rangers also brought over 3,000 Texan desperados to justice,

including the train robber Sam Bass (in 1878) and the gone-to-the-bad gunfighter Wesley Hardin. Hardin was reputed to have killed thirty-one men, but was captured single-handed by Ranger John B. Armstrong, wielding a long-barrelled Colt .45, shouting 'Texas, by God!'

The legislation of 1874 was a defining moment in the history of the force, whose members were now officially officers of the peace, rather than fighting men serving in a semi-military organization. Despite this, if a Ranger was fighting an outside force, such as Mexicans or Indians, he continued to be judged as a soldier. But when he was enforcing the Texan criminal law, he was considered a detective or policeman. The Ranger's role often involved bringing the rule of law to the massive Texan ranches, combating fence cutters and cattle rustlers. The Rangers' authority was acknowledged state wide, without reference to city or county boundaries.

Left and Below: The newly enclosed Texan ranges often fell victim to fence cutters and rustlers. The Rangers were their only defense against these miscreants.

Both below: Senior Ranger Captain Frank Hamer and his colleague Manny Gault finally tracked down Bonnie and Clyde Parker, after 102 days. The Rangers had hoped to take the dangerous duo alive, but gunned them down when they reached for their weapons.

Between 1894 and 1895, the Rangers scouted 173,381 miles, made 676 arrests, returned 2,856 head of cattle to their rightful owners, assisted the civil authorities on 162 occasions, and were brought in to guard jails thirteen times.

The Frontier Battalion nomenclature was abolished in 1901, the name fading into history along with the frontier itself. The Rangers were now seen purely as a law enforcement agency; an elite group of officers brought in to support local lawmen. Unfortunately, the Rangers had been so effective that they now seemed redundant. Their numbers declined to a mere four companies of twenty men each.

This tiny force was completely overwhelmed by the dramatic events at the beginning of the twentieth century – prohibition, the Mexican Revolution, and the Texan oil boom to name but three. Rather than beef the force up, it was even further depleted to four companies of only fifteen men.

But it gradually became apparent to the State legislators that Texas badly needed an elite force to handle some of its toughest crimes. In 1935, the Rangers became the cream of the Texas Department of Public Safety (which also contained the Texan Highway Patrol). This force was the true forbear of the modern-day Texas Ranger, developing more modern and subtle approaches to the sophisticated crime of the modern era.

The Rangers gradually swapped their horses for cars, responding to a different criminal profile. One of the most famous Rangers of this era, Senior Ranger Captain Frank Hamer, trailed Bonnie and Clyde for 102 days, together with his Ranger colleague Manny Gault. The Rangers finally caught up with the dangerous duo in Louisiana's Bienville Parish, setting up an ambush on a rural Louisiana road. The Rangers had planned to take the couple alive, but gunned them down when they reached for their weapons. They ended

Left: The Rangers were
active in enforcing
prohibition between 1920
and 1933. They located and
destroyed many stills.

the pair's killing spree of at least thirteen murders, including police officers.

A falling off in standards took place in the 1920s, when Governor Ferguson allowed some men to be inducted in the service who were not worthy of the honor, including some ex-convicts. This indignity resulted in forty Rangers, including Hamer, resigning. Between 1920 and 1933, National Prohibition forbade the sale of alcohol, and Rangers worked closely with Federal agents to destroy stills and confiscate illegal alcohol smuggled in from Mexico. They co-operated in shutting down liquor distribution networks, illegal gambling dens, and speakeasies.

A general cleanup of the service was instigated in 1934, following a Texas Senate inquiry. This recommended the establishment of the Department of Public Safety, an institution that still survives to this day, which would operate the Ranger service. This was to be cut down to a meagre 36 men, but would benefit from state-of-the-art crime-fighting techniques and a vastly improved communications network. In these early years as part of the DPS, Rangers were

Above: Always a semi-military force, the Rangers took a strong interest in weaponry.

furnished with an updated version of the Colt .45, together with a lever action Winchester .30 rifle. They still had to provide their own horse and saddle, though these were now driven long distances in state-supplied horse trailers.

During World War II, the Rangers were part of the internal Texan security network, screening air raid warning training films and tracking down escaped German POWs. By 1945, the force was again on the increase, to 51 men. Their duties continued to evolve, and during the 1950s, Rangers

Right and below: Through Pinkerton's good offices, and intelligence network, Lincoln survived long enough to be inaugurated as President. He blamed himself for the final, successful attempt on the President's life, as he had left Washington by this time.

Railroad, whose attorney was none other than the young Abraham Lincoln. In HANGING WOMAN CREEK, L'Amour describes how Pinkerton man Jim Fargo is trying to track down the murderous Van Bokkelen, to the surprise of main character Barney Pike. Pike says that he thought 'Pinks usually only hunted train robbers and the like.' It was certainly true that this formed a good part of the Agency's early work. Pike later reflects that Pinkerton agents are also hired by cattle ranchers, or by companies like Wells Fargo. This (rather controversially) suggests that contemporaries believed Pinkerton agents were only interested in law enforcement when financial concerns are involved. Interestingly, though, Jim Fargo is also a deputy US marshal.

As well as acute powers of detection, Pinkerton offered high standards of ethical behavior by himself and his operatives. He was an excellent PR man, coining the company slogan 'We never sleep' and its trademark 'eye.' This emblem is the root of our modern phrase 'private eye.' The agency itself was colloquially known as 'The Eye.' All his agents were expected to maintain high personal standards, and he handpicked them himself. Some of the famous original 'Pinks' were George H. Bangs, Francis Warner, and Kate Warne. Kate was the first female detective in America, and her 1856 appointment was particularly groundbreaking. The police didn't employ women officers until 1891, and didn't use women as investigators until 1903.

Some Pinks were reformed criminals, and used their knowledge of lawbreaking to assist their detective work. In THE MAN CALLED NOON, J.B. Rimes turns out to be a Pinkerton agent. L'Amour describes him as an ex-outlaw, who had been recruited by the Agency to catch a train robber. But Rimes is now firmly on the side of the law, and ends up by bringing the vicious Peg Cullane to justice.

From the very beginning, the Agency used the most up-to-date technology to facilitate its investigations, employing telegraph and weapons experts. Pinkerton was also an early exponent of psychology. He once hired a double for a murdered bank clerk to stalk the perpetrator until the man completely broke down, convinced that his victim was haunting him. By the 1870s, the Agency had the world's largest collection of mug shots and an extensive database of criminals. Pinkerton's methods were progressively adopted by the police force itself.

The Agency gradually became a household name, particularly after its involvement in a series of high profile cases, such as the Adams Express Job, where Allan was able to return $39,515 of a stolen $50,000.

But perhaps Pinkerton's most famous coupe was his defeat of an assassination plot to kill his old friend Abraham Lincoln, the newly elected President. Lincoln's strong pro-abolitionist stance during his campaign had earned him a good deal of hostility in the South, and there were serious concerns that civil war would break out if he were to be elected. While guarding the route of the Philadelphia, Wilmington, and Baltimore Railroad – the main rail artery to the South – Pinkerton agents picked up intelligence about a plot for a Confederate group, the Knights of the Golden Circle to murder the incumbent President at Baltimore's Calvert Rail Station. Even the local chief of police was implicated in the conspiracy. But Pinkerton managed to spirit 'Abe' away, and save his life long enough to be sworn in.

Later in that year of 1861, the dreaded civil war did indeed break out. Convinced by his own experiences as to the efficacy of intelligence work, President Lincoln summoned Pinkerton to the capital. He called upon him to organize a secret service in Washington to flush out Confederate spies. In effect, this was the first ever government-sanctioned spy ring in the US. Pinkerton employed some of his most trusted agents on this work, including Kate Warne, who divided her time between Virginia and Tennessee, posing as a Southern belle. In fact, women agents were used on both sides. One of the Confederate agents flushed out by Pinkerton's spies was Rose O'Neil Greenhow who had passed vital plans to the South. Once exposed, she was lucky to escape hanging. Pinkerton agent Elizabeth Baker successfully discovered the existence of a Confederate-built early submarine. This information effectively prevented the Confederacy from

As well as acute powers of detection, Pinkerton offered high standards of ethical behavior by himself and his operatives

Colt Buntline Special

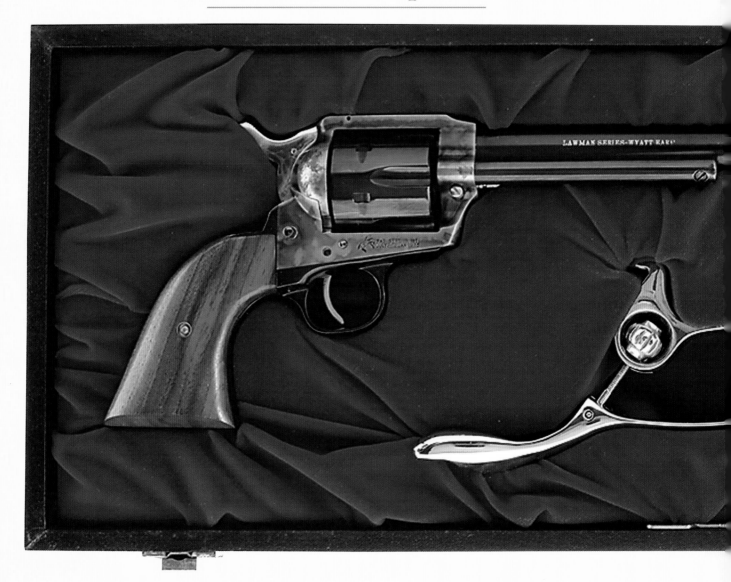

An exciting innovation to the Colt Single Action appeared at the Philadelphia Centennial Exhibition of 1876, when the weapon was offered with a 16 inch barrel and a skeleton shoulder stock. Only thirty examples were originally offered. The gun acquired its legendary association with Wyatt Earp when (it was claimed) dime novelist Ned Buntline (Edward Judson) ordered five Colt Special .45 revolvers to equip the Dodge City Peace Commission, of whom Earp was one. This is how the guns got their name, the Buntline Specials. It is not known if Earp actually carried a Special, but Buckskin Frank Leslie, a Tombstone gambler and

bartender, ordered a 10 inch version in 1881. This was the year of the Earp brothers' famous gunfight at the O.K. Corral.

Clearly these experimental modifications would have turned the single action into a very useful weapon. Fired down a sixteen-inch barrel, the .45 cartridges would have been extremely accurate and have had great stopping power at range. The nickel-plated skeleton stock would have meant that the shootist could have held the gun extremely steady and would have enabled them to take careful aim before squeezing the trigger.

The gun could also be fired without the stock, and the extra weight of the barrel would have ironed out any tendency to kick from the extra length.

The gun went on to be manufactured for many years after 1876, and is still available in presentation cases like the one shown.

Louis L'Amour cites Wyatt Earp as the gunman to beat in many of his Western novels, and he has helped to keep alive the legend of the West's greatest gunman.

SPECIFICATIONS

Caliber: 0.45 inch

Length of barrel: 16 inches

Barrel shape: Round

Finish: Blue/casehardened

Grips: Walnut

Action: Single Action Revolver

Year of manufacture: 1876

Manufacturer: Colt

Above: A modern reproduction of this legendary arm, complete with skeleton stock and silk lined presentation case. Such weapons are highly prized by collectors.

The Civil War

'A house divided against itself cannot stand. I believe that government cannot endure, permanently half slave and half free.' LINCOLN

Below: *(Oval)* The Battle of Shiloh. *(Bottom picture)* A stone bridge on the Warrenton turnpike near Bull Run. It became a symbol of Union losses.

The Civil War was ignited by the issue of slavery, but with the secession of several pro-slavery Southern states, an even bigger issue became paramount – the preservation of the Union itself. When Lincoln became President, control of the nation's government passed to the North for the first time in several generations, and hostilities seemed inevitable. When it came, the conflict touched almost every American family in some way or another,

including that of Louis L'Amour, whose grandfather fought in the War. The ripples of the conflict can be felt in many of his Western novels, and in the lives of both his real and imaginary characters.

Although much of the West was left pretty well unscathed by the actual fighting, the spark that ignited the nation-wide conflagration happened in the territory in the fall of 1855. The new states of Kansas and Missouri were bitterly divided by the issue of slavery, and this led to the murder of an abolitionist settler by his pro-slavery neighbor. This in turn resulted in a miniature 'civil war' between the 'free-soiler' abolitionists and the pro-slavery movement. This preceded the events of the nationwide conflict by several years. In fact, some of the bitterest fighting of the War, between the so-called Jayhawkers and Bushwhackers, tore the region apart. Their vicious and barbaric methods were epitomized by such men as the brutal 'Bloody Bill' Quantrill, for whom Jesse James fought. His specialty was the murder and pillage of innocent civilians and their homes.

As the major hostilities broke out, other Western states became part of the theater of war. Texas and Arkansas declared for the Confederacy. Kansas was on the Unionist side. Missouri was a border slave state. But loyalties did not necessarily follow state lines, and like many parents, Eve Prescott Rawlings worried that her sons could end up on different sides of the conflict. Her mountain man husband,

Linus, died at the great battle of Shiloh in April 1862, where he and his son Zeb fought on the side of Grant and Sherman against Johnston's confederate forces. In a cinematic moment typical of L'Amour, Zeb Rawlings prevents a Texan from killing Grant, and unwittingly turns his back on the dead body of his father. He returns home, only to find the graves of both of his parents. As for many, sorrow is his underlying motive for the trek West.

Despite that fact that Valverde in New Mexico saw the farthest westerly battle of the War, virtually every aspect of Western life was affected by the conflict in some way or other. For example, many Plains Indians became swept into the hostilities. Although Lincoln attempted to persuade the tribes to remain neutral, the withdrawal of the US military was seized upon as an opportunity by warlike tribes

Left: Brigadier General J. E. B. Stuart, a great Confederate commander.

Below: Colonel Michael Corcoran and the officers of the 69th New York State Militia gather around an artillery piece at Fort Corcoran.

like the Apache and Navajo who began a campaign of raids against frontier settlers.

Lawfulness in general was often a victim of the conflict, as many officers, including those of the Texas Rangers, were obliged to join the military forces on both sides. Once the fighting was over, there were a lot of experienced men available to work on the side of justice, and just as many dispossessed desperados ready to break the law.

The Sheridan doctrine of destroying confederate property, so that 'The people must be left with nothing but their eyes to weep with,' meant that the economy of the South was ruined. Texas was left particularly battle-scarred and impoverished. Ironically though, the thriving industrial towns of the North, such as Chicago, were hungry for meat, and Texan beef was in huge demand. Cattle were selling at as much as $30 to $40 a head in the northern meat markets. This high demand gave cattle entrepreneurs like Charles Goodnight and his ilk an opening they did not fail to exploit.

When Robert E. Lee surrendered on April 9, 1865, victory celebrations were held all over the West. For the frontier region, the end of the war heralded a new wave of immigrants. The collapse of the Southern economy, the loss of many personal fortunes, and general war fatigue, encouraged many to make their way West for a fresh start – just as the Sackett brothers do in THE DAYBREAKERS. Not only men braved the challenge of the frontier. In THE CHEROKEE TRAIL, Mary Breydon has been burnt out of her Virginia home and widowed, and needs to make a new life for herself and her little daughter. She becomes the manager of a stagecoach station, and turns it into a vital stop on America's Westward journey.

At the cost of over 620,000 lives, the Union had been saved, and America was restored to nationhood. The democratic Republic, created in 1776, survived. But the victorious Lincoln had precious little time to access the harrowing cost of the War. He lost his life to a murderous Confederate Marylander, John Wilkes Booth, who was incensed that former black slaves would now become citizens.

Opposite page: The field at Gettysburg, scene of the most costly military action ever to take place on American soil.

Above: President Ulysses S. Grant, one of the greatest Union commanders.

Left: The Civil War created the greatest schism in American society since the foundation of the Republic. Sometimes North against South led to brother against brother.

Wells Fargo & Co.

Opposite page: Wells Fargo stagecoaches often rode with a shotgun outrider for protection. The company established their business to serve all the frontiers people of the Western territories.

Wells Fargo was one of the great institutions of the West, and was a positive force for the civilizing of the Wild Frontier. Its very name conjures a thrilling image of a six-horse stagecoach loaded with gold, thundering across the romantic plains landscape. Louis L'Amour clearly recognized the importance of the company, and refers to it often in his Western novels. In fact, its activities became part of the fabric of the American West, serving people of every background and profession, and actively seeking to control lawlessness, although as Clyde points out in THE EMPTY LAND, 'Wells Fargo does not build towns nor enforce the law… except along the stage routes.' Henry Wells and William Fargo founded the company in 1852, and the company's first office was set up in downtown San Francisco at 420 Montgomery Street, right in the heart of the tent city of the '49ers. The new company offered banking (buying gold, selling bank drafts) and express, secure carriage for all kinds of cargo, especially gold dust and bullion from the newly sunk mines. Right from the beginning, there was also a thread of altruism in the company culture. Wells Fargo offered their services to all 'men, women, or children, rich or poor, white or black.' Indeed, they ran their business for all the settlers and frontiers people of the West, including blacks,

Below: Documented Wells Fargo Hammer Shotgun.

Right: Wells Fargo issued all their operatives with recognizable badges, and their logo became a symbol of civilization moving westwards.

whites, and Spanish-speaking Hispanics. William Wells was also an early proponent of sexual equality, later founding Wells College for Women in New York with the slogan, 'Give her the opportunity!' Several women were agents by the 1880s, sometimes taking over from their husbands as company employees when they were widowed. Veterans of the US Army have also worked for the company for over 150 years, helping to build the great overland stage lines and founding the financial service aspect of the company.

Integrity was a great factor in the success of the business and Wells Fargo agents often became highly respected figures in the new towns and volatile mining settlements of the West.

Below: Madison Larkin was a Wells Fargo Messenger and shotgun guard, and would have worked for one or other of the local agents. He is photographed at Phoenix in 1877.

They were recruited from well-respected members of the community, including storekeepers and attorneys, and were each given a certificate of appointment by the company. As well as the Express service, the agents also offered basic banking and financial services.

The company started their overland stagecoach line in the 1860s, and was also partly responsible for the Butterfield

Overland Mail Company established in 1858 (which they later took over). They sent the mail by the fastest means possible, stagecoach, steamship, railroad, pony rider or telegraph, and their operatives often brought the mail through at dreadful personal risk. Wells Fargo also employed detectives to investigate fraud and any other illegal practices in connection with their business, together

Left: The Wells Fargo stagecoaches were often subject to hold ups, from desperados attracted by the gold and valuables they often conveyed, but armed guards usually protected these shipments.

Below: Wells Fargo inscription above the barrels of the Wells Fargo Remington shotgun featured on page 152.

with armed escorts and shotgun riders to discourage theft and hold ups. They were reputed to carry cut down shotguns, which were easy to conceal under the seat of a wagon, and lethal at close range.

This modus operandi daunted many would-be villains. Ben Curry's gang (SON OF A WANTED MAN) didn't risk stage hold ups carrying large shipments of money or bullion precisely because these consignments would have shotgun guards. German Bayles (THE MAN

CALLED NOON) rode as a Wells Fargo shotgun guard before going to the bad, and 'His activities had seesawed back and forth on both sides of the law.' L'Amour character J.B. Rimes (THE MAN CALLED

Winchester 1873

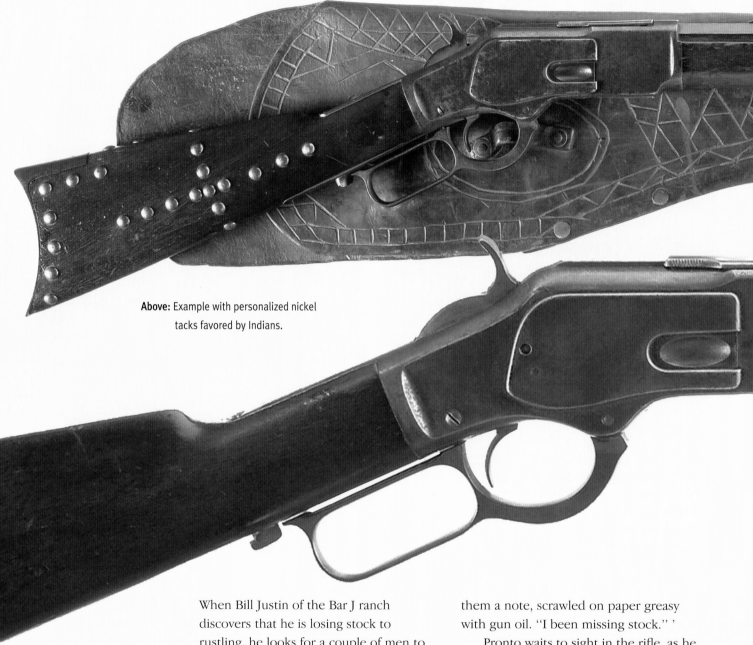

Above: Example with personalized nickel tacks favored by Indians.

Above: The heavy duty steel frame and receiver allowed the use of heavier center fire ammunition.

When Bill Justin of the Bar J ranch discovers that he is losing stock to rustling, he looks for a couple of men to keep watch at his HANGING WOMAN CREEK line camp. Pronto Pike and Eddie Holt are two drifters looking for a job, and fit the bill perfectly. Their new boss equips them with a wagon full of supplies, guns, and ammunition. Eddie is the first to discover the weaponry: ' "Pronto you come see this here." What he was showing me were two brand-new Winchester 73s and boxes with about 500 rounds of ammunition. And with

them a note, scrawled on paper greasy with gun oil. "I been missing stock." '

Pronto waits to sight in the rifle, as he is dubious of hitting anything with the Colt .44s packed in the wagon. He says that he has never owned a handgun because they are too expensive, even second-hand. He has been wont to carry a Winchester 'but that was a meat gun, and a man never knew when he would have to brush off a scalp-hunting Sioux.' Along with the Colt Peacemaker, the Winchester shared the reputation of being the 'gun that won the west.'

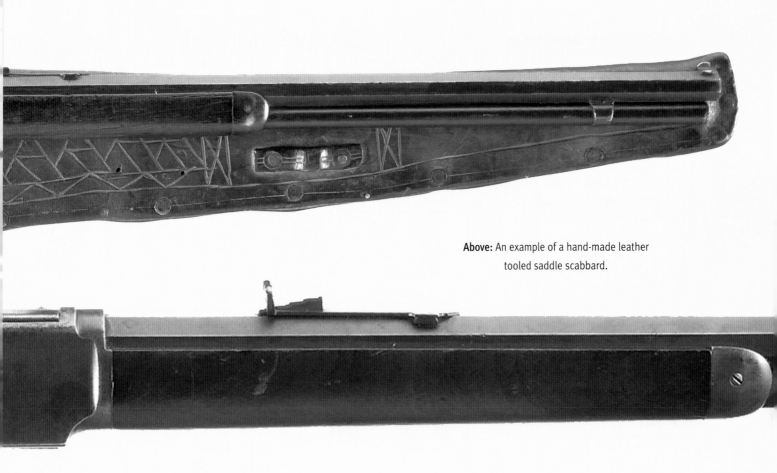

Above: An example of a hand-made leather tooled saddle scabbard.

In reality, the frontier was all over by 1890 and the gun remained in production until 1919. This put the greater part of the model output well outside the period on which its fame rests.

The 1873 was an advance over the 1866 model, as its frame and receiver were made from stronger, lighter steel instead of brass. Gone was the pretty 'yellow-boy' look. This enabled the use of the more powerful center fire cartridge designated as .44-40. This was a .44 inch caliber bullet propelled by a cartridge containing 40 grains of black powder. It was a potent combination.

Colt launched the Peacemaker the same year and wisely offered the gun in the same range of calibers as the Winchester rifle. This meant that the ammunition was interchangeable and a man needed to carry only one sort of cartridge.

Above: Classic Winchester lines make this one of the most recognizable Western arms.

SPECIFICATIONS

Caliber: 0.44-40 inch

Length of barrel: 24 inches

Barrel shape: octagonal

Finish: blue/casehardened

Grips: Walnut

Action: 15 shot lever action

Year of manufacture: 1890

Manufacturer: Winchester Repeating Arms Company, New Haven, Connecticut

We show two models, both with 24 inch barrels. The second has a tooled leather scabbard. This gun was the property of a cowboy, Hug Brown, and it bears his initials.

Colt Revolving Shotgun

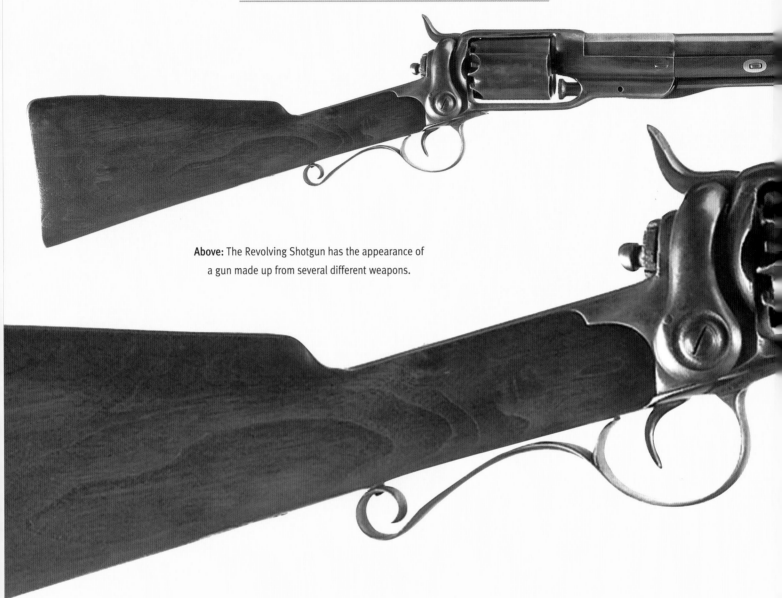

Above: The Revolving Shotgun has the appearance of a gun made up from several different weapons.

Above: The heavy duty hammer and reinforced octagonal breech give testament to the solidity of Colt's engineering.

Louis L'Amour really demonstrates his knowledge of Western armaments in UTAH BLAINE, and the book is a rich source of exotic weaponry. During a nighttime standoff at the Bar B Ranch the three defenders Utah Blaine, Dan Timm, and Rip Coker 'advertise' the prowess of their weapons for the benefit of the opposition. Rip Coker, an ornery hand who has thrown in his lot with Blaine despite the odds against him, uses positive psychology to outwit Russ Nevers and his men. He is armed with a Winchester rifle, which he manages to pass off as a Colt Revolving Shotgun in the dark. 'Wish you gents

would make up your minds to die,' Coker commented casually. 'This here Colt shotgun is loadin' my arms down.' If it had been the Colt, it would have been a big gun. The gun barrels were between 30 inch (with a round profile) and a massive 36 inch (when the profile was part octagonal). The cylinder held four chambers of 10 gauge shot, which would retain its velocity for a reasonable distance when discharged down a 3/4 inch, three foot long barrel! Rather nervous in the dark, Russ Nevers quietly reflects that 'a blast from a shotgun did awful things to a man, and this gun held four shells. And

Above: Oval Side nail cover is a detail which harks back to the days of flintlock arms.

SPECIFICATIONS

Caliber: 0.75 inch

Length of barrel: 36 inches

Barrel shape: Part octagonal

Finish: Blue, casehardened

Grips: Walnut

Action: Single action four-shot revolver

Year of manufacture: 1855

Manufacturer: Colonel Colt, Hartford, Connecticut

The weapon owed its existence to the much earlier 1839 Paterson revolving shotgun. In the early days, Samuel Colt believed that rifles, carbines, and shotguns would be the mainstay of his business and set out to apply his revolving mechanism to these types of armaments. The Paterson had a six shot chamber of smaller caliber, .62 of an inch.

The later model was patented on September 10th, 1850 and became the Colt Model 1855. There was a flurry of competition about this time with revolving long arms being introduced by manufacturers such as Roper, Cherington, Porter, and James Warner.

At the time, 'revolving' seemed to be the answer to repeat-shooting firearms, and became so for handguns for the rest of the century. But for rifles and shotguns, the future lay with the Henry and the underlever action of the later Winchesters.

there was the possibility of reloads before they could get to him.' Indeed Colt produced charger flasks to enable all four chambers to be reloaded at once. In terms of rate of fire, this gun was not one to be underestimated.

At this time, the population of the West was very fluid, with incomers restlessly moving about, searching for land and opportunity. It became scattered with abandoned 'ghost' towns. The coming (or not) of the railroad could also make or break a town. Marshal 'Borden Chantry glanced out the kitchen window toward the train station. When the tracks were built through town they fortunately passed within fifty yards of his home' (SON OF A WANTED MAN), but the train also attracts criminality.

If they developed, the towns went on

Above and right: A re-creation of a typical general store, with a wonderful interior replete with everything a frontiersperson could need – besom brooms, oven paddles, salt pork (in the barrels), dried meat, grain, flour, molasses, oil lamps, pitchers, pans and some dainty china.

Chance, The Bon-Ton Restaurant, the Discovery, and the Treasure Vault.

Coburn knows that these frontier towns could (and did) evaporate like a puff of smoke, if their water, gold, or luck ran out. 'I like to look at new towns,' he says 'to wonder how long they will last.'

to cater for the Westerners' every need. One of the first of these was communication, and a feeling of being a part of the civilized world – whether or not this was actually true. Like a Wells Fargo office, a local newspaper gave a flimsy new town a feeling of solidity and permanence. In UTAH BLAINE, Ralston

Left: Most towns needed a sawmill for house-building lumber.

Above: Of course, there were also less usual items on sale on the typical western high street, including gun powder.

Forbes owns the newspaper at Red Creek, and uses it to see justice done in the town. In Confusion, 'the press' arrives soon after the town gets started: 'Sturdevant Fife is coming up the trail with his printing press. He's a law and order man, and he runs his newspaper with a sawed-off shotgun on his desk.' Fife is shown setting the type for his first front page in Confusion, ' "… Men Killed on the First Day." I'm leaving the number open. The day ain't over yet.' Fife had promised the original owner of his press to 'tell the truth, the whole truth and nothin' but the truth.' Like Ralston Forbes, he ends up wielding a gun rather than a pen, in support of Marshal Coburn.

A panorama of re-created buildings found in a typical frontier town. They reflect the interests of the townsfolk, and the raw nature of western life.

1

2

4

3

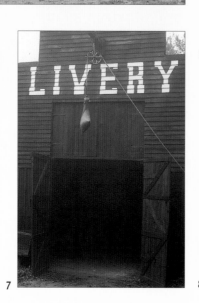

5

6

7

8

9

10

12

13

11

1 The apothecary.
2 The Cantina.
3 The Lone Star Saloon.
4 The Town Marshal's office.
5 The office of the Lonesome Dove Mining Company.
6 The Western Union Telegraph Office.
7 The livery yard.
8 The Texas Rangers' office.
9 The Gunsmith.
10 The town hotel.
11 Wells Fargo Office.
12 The church meeting house.
13 The town well.
14 The bank.
15 A photographer sets up his tripod in front of the marshal's office.

14

15

Above: The railroad became hugely important to the cattle industry. Many animals were shipped East on the hoof.

Right: A typical frontier hotel and its guests.

Red Creek, the town at the centre of the action in UTAH BLAINE is the other archetypal Western settlement, whose economy depends on cattle. 'It was a one-street town with hitching rails before most of the buildings. The bank was conveniently across from the livery stable. Beyond the stable was the blacksmith shop, facing a general store across the street.' The store was at the heart of the town, and was fundamental to its survival, as well as being a social place to visit. Newt Clyde says of Gage, Confusion's understandably nervous storekeeper, 'When he leaves, the town is finished.' 'There was a scattering of other buildings and behind them, rows of residences, some of the yards fenced, most of them bare and untended.' Utah eats in the enticingly named Shoo-Fly Restaurant. L'Amour evokes the town very simply, but we recognize it and the people we meet there. They are both essential Westerners.

Abilene was the first true 'cow town' in the US, and is featured in L'Amour. Illinois businessman J.C. McCoy established the cattle market there in 1867. Over 600,000 heads were driven into the town in a single year, and were then railroaded on the hoof to the Eastern cities. 'Abilene in 1871 was a booming town, but the boom was almost over… (it was) wild and woolly, and it was loud,' full of dusty cowboys and drivers. Abilene's town authorities brought in Wild Bill Hickok as Marshal to try and

tame the town. But although he successfully introduced gun control, he failed to establish the kind of peace the townsfolk longed for. They decided to forgo the income from the cattle drives, and the business went to other stops on the line, such as Ellsworth, Newton, and Dodge City itself, the last and most wicked of the Kansas cow towns.

In fact, the 'cow town' tag wasn't considered to be entirely flattering. Towns with other roles liked to point these out, 'Miles City wasn't just a cow town, for Fort Keogh was close by with around a thousand men – soldiers and civilian employees.'

The facilities of a typical Western town reflect the diverse requirements of the townsfolk. The usual range of services included the Assay Office (to register land and stake claims), the livery stables, a hotel, various saloons, a bank, general store, Wells Fargo office, gunsmith, barber, Marshal's office (which might also accommodate the town jail), blacksmith, restaurant, the town well, Western Union Telegraph office, a Texas Rangers office, an apothecary, dentist, school house, newspaper office and printing shop, town

photographer, church meeting house and, of course, the town cemetery.

Perhaps the depth of Louis L'Amour's fascination with these frontier towns and settlements is best shown by his intention to recreate a Western town of 1865 – Shalako. 'Where the borders of Utah, Arizona, New Mexico, and Colorado meet.' In the very heart of the West, 'Historically authentic from whistle to well, it will be a live, operating town, as well as a movie location and tourist attraction.' Sadly, this ambition was never realized in his lifetime.

Above and left: Many towns were abandoned when their gold, silver, water, or luck ran out, and became atmospheric 'ghost' settlements.

Remington Double Barrel Model 1889 shotgun

In SON OF A WANTED MAN, we are introduced to Doc Sawyer, a character who is mistaken for a gambler by the sheriff. His respectable dress sets him apart from the cowhands. It is possible that L'Amour based the character – to some extent – on the famous Doc Holliday, who is also mentioned in his work. Holliday was a member of Wyatt Earp's Dodge City Peace Commission. His weapon of choice was usually a shotgun, and Earp described him as 'the nerviest, fastest, deadliest man with a six-gun I ever saw.' He was also a professional gambler and killer. Doc Sawyer is a much nicer man, who although tough is not violent for the sake of it. Mike Bastian, for whom the novel is named, finds the Doc holding four of bad guy Kerb Perrin's men 'backed against the wall,' courtesy of his shotgun.

Western Shotguns were specially designed to create respect in close quarter fights. They had shortened barrels to allow for

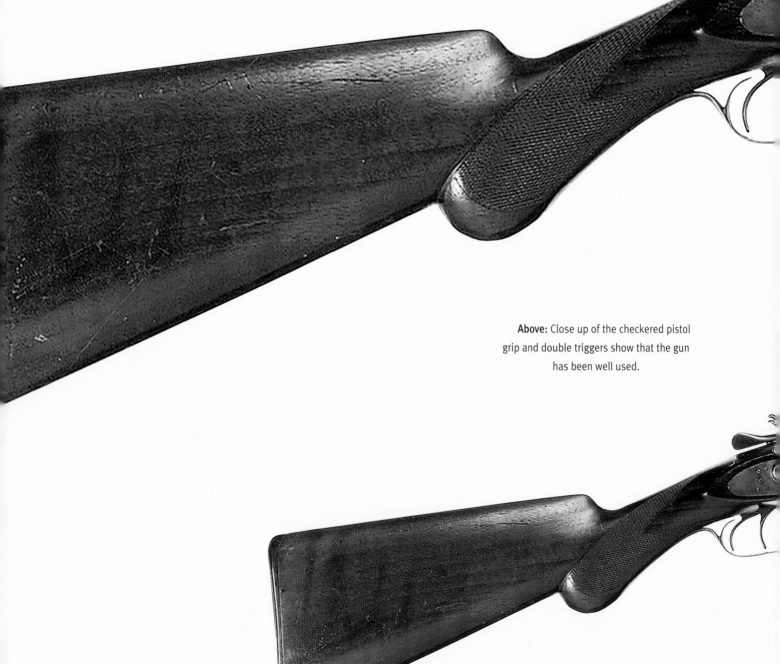

Above: Close up of the checkered pistol grip and double triggers show that the gun has been well used.

SPECIFICATIONS

Caliber: 12 gauge

Length of barrel: 18 inches

Barrel shape: Round

Finish: Browned steel

Grips: Walnut, checkered with pistol grip

Action: Breech loading double barrel

Year of manufacture: 1889

Manufacturer: Remington Arms Company, Ilion, New York

maneuverability and a widespread shot pattern. To this day, criminals 'saw off' barrels to achieve the same effect. At close quarters Doc Sawyer has the drop on four of Perrin's men simply because a single twitch of his fingers would send them all to hell in pieces.

The guns had a pistol grip stock for firing from the hip and external hammers for quick cocking. They were particularly popular with law enforcement agents and stagecoach guards.

Above: The barrels have been shortened to give a more concentrated blast at close range.

Winchester Model 1887 Lever Action Shotgun

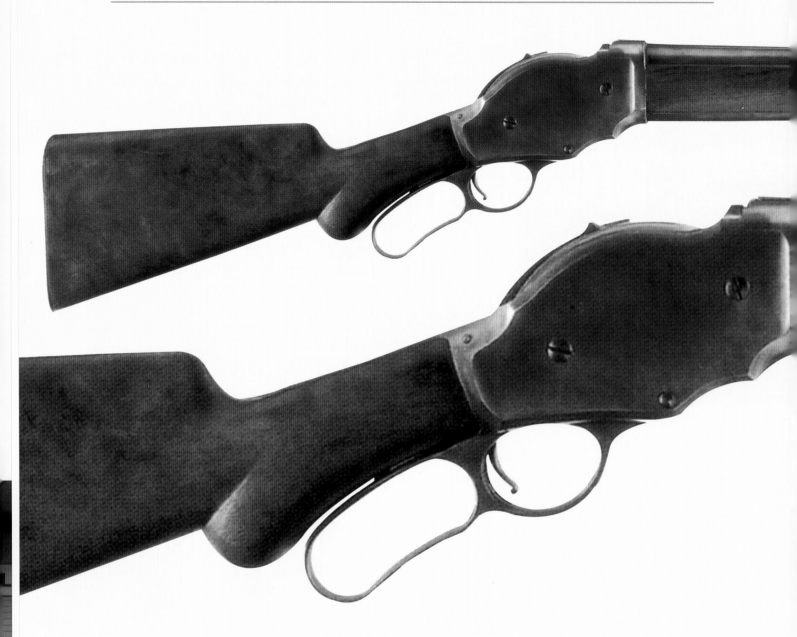

The 1887 Shotgun was hardly the most elegant of the company's weapons.

In the final years of the Frontier, weapons evolved into more deadly versions of the earlier arms. Gone was the primitive percussion system, which took time to load, and muzzle-loaders that suffered from variable powder charges and poor gas sealing. The center-fire brass cartridge and double action had made the revolver a much more serious weapon. Outlaws like Billy the Kid caught on very quickly to the latest models, such as the Colt Lightning and Frontier types. Rifles were also now available with reliable repeating mechanisms. Similarly, shotgun design had to move with the times.

In Louis L'Amour's Western novels, the plot often calls for a shotgun to pin down opposing forces of overwhelming strength. Shotguns also appear in the role of protecting jails or bullion shipments where their close-range devastation would deter potential hold ups. But to this point they suffered from the serious drawback of having only a two shot

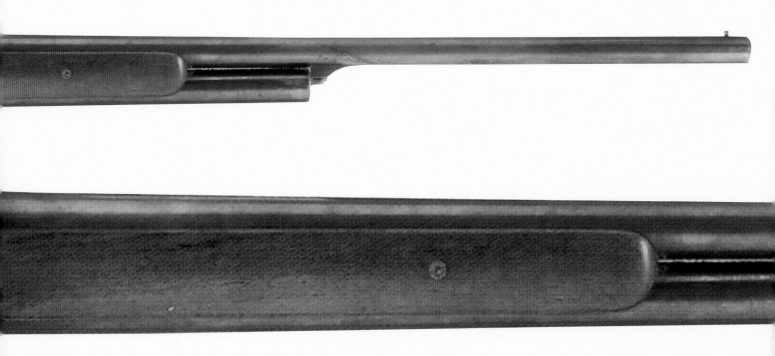

capacity in double barrel form. Colt had developed an early version of the revolving shotgun but this never really took off. It was left to Winchester to develop a lever action shotgun to reflect their successful rifles. Designed by John Browning, the 1887 shotgun was chunky and aggressive looking – just right for a weapon designed to intimidate. It had a five-shot magazine in a tube positioned under the barrel, and was available in 10 and 12-gauge. The barrel lengths of the gun ranged from 32 inches to a 'sawn-off' 20 inches for crowd control (or criminal purposes).

The gun was a favorite weapon with the Texas Rangers, and it continued in production until 1920. A weapon of this kind was used by Texan lawman, George W. Scarborough, who killed the assassin of John Wesley Hardin – John Selman – in an alley. The outlaw Kid Curry in turn, murdered Scarborough. Violent times indeed!

Above: Close-up of the familiar Winchester underlever action and 5 shot magazine tube slung under the barrel.

SPECIFICATIONS

Caliber: 12-Gauge

Length of barrel: 28 inches

Barrel shape: Round

Finish: blue/casehardened

Grips: Walnut

Action: 5 shot lever action

Year of manufacture: 1887

Manufacturer: Winchester Repeating Arms Co., New Haven, Connecticut

Western Women

Despite Barney Pike's assertion (in HANGING WOMAN CREEK) that the West is 'hell on horses and women,' Louis L'Amour's heroines often seem more poised and focused than their male equivalents.

From the start of the migration to the West, the position of frontier women was substantially different from that of women in the East. Women in the West represented a highly valued asset in short supply, and this was reflected in the greater status and freedom they enjoyed. Utah was the first territory to enfranchise women, while California was the first state to legislate for married women to retain ownership of their property. This was partly because this was the Mexican tradition, and partly to attract wealthy women to make the move West to get married.

Louis L'Amour describes a very wide spectrum of women in his Western novels, and most of his female characters are very successful in adapting to this new environment. The facts of Western settlement seem to bear this out. Although it is recognized that very few women initiated the trek to the West, once there, the vast majority of the women settlers proved that they were the equals, or even the superiors, of men in trials of bravery and fortitude. For instance, at the end of the appalling winter endured by the Donner party, snowed in the Sierra, the survivors were reduced to cannibalism. But all the women survived while eight out of ten men perished.

Several female L'Amour characters are also credited with out-performing their male counterparts. In TO THE FAR BLUE MOUNTAINS, Barney Sackett describes the redoubtable Lila (his wife Abigail's maid) as being 'worth three men.' She takes a full part in their adventures, and uses her culinary skills to bring an entire pirate ship to heel. As she says of herself 'Wherever a man can go, I can go... I shall be no burden,' and her brother fully endorses this, saying 'As for the savages, if they molest my sister, God have mercy upon them, for she will not!' Cohan similarly describes the hard women of the gold rush towns as being 'tough enough to whip any two men in camp, and ready to do it.'

But we feel that the women L'Amour himself admires the most are his rather more attractive 'love interest' characters. Throughout the canon of his work, his good women, the ones that his heroes fall for, are almost universally described as 'ladies.' According to L'Amour, being a 'lady' has nothing to do with background or upbringing, but is rather a combination of innate qualities: modesty, strength, intelligence, beauty, and self-possession. As Barney Sackett tells Abigail, 'Wherever she grows up... your daughter would be a lady.' Ann Farley, the love interest in HANGING WOMAN CREEK, comes all the way from Ireland to assist her brother Philo in his frontier life. Pike's first impression of her is typical in these circumstances, 'She was a lady, every inch of her... and there was something clean and fine about her that made a man look twice.' In CATLOW, the willful Cordelia Burton is described as having 'courage, and a cool, quiet strength, but above all she was a lady.'

Although many L'Amour women demonstrate their capabilities, their need to do so often results from the illness, incapacity, or death of men. Mary Blake is

Right: A lovely photograph of family life in the West in the early twentieth century, a family swing outside their log cabin.

forced to run her B-Bar ranch following the murder of her father, but she is ultimately dependent on Utah Blaine to retain her property. Fan Davidge becomes beholden to Ruble Noon in similar circumstances. When Barney Sackett falls seriously ill, Abigail takes over his role at the helm of their ship 'She who knew much of men and ships, and in this my illness, took over. When there was doubt, she resolved it, when there was a decision to be made, she made it.' Despite this share of the action, the qualities that the L'Amour women show (such as loyalty and courage) often seem to be a result of their love for men, such as Angie in UTAH BLAINE who keeps up her lovely home in honor of her dead father, while Abigail submits herself to the danger of a transatlantic voyage to stand by her man. L'Amour is also careful to demonstrate that even very brave, active women do not necessarily become mannish or hardened. Dru Ragan insists on bringing a rifle when she rides with Mike Bastian to save her sister from the clutches of the depraved Ducrow, but he allows her to cry with fear.

L'Amour also shows how a woman can be sexually liberated without losing her feminine charm. Several L'Amour heroines actively choose their own partners, rather than passively waiting to be chosen. In fact, there are several instances where male heroes, courageous in every other way, aren't brave enough to offer themselves to the women of their choice. Eve Prescott chooses Linus Rawlings to be 'her man,' and initiates their courtship, while Madge Healy proposes to Matt Coburn. He is definitely the 'man' of the relationship, but she has the economic power. Neither does L'Amour underestimate the intelligence of women. Ben Cowan is opposed to Diego Recalde's 'Mexican' analysis of Rosita Calderon as being too intelligent. His more 'American viewpoint' can appreciate that a clever wife would be an asset to the politically ambitious officer. Nor do L'Amour's male characters often get an opportunity to deceive their women. Lillith Prescott is immediately aware that Cleve Van Valen is attracted to her, initially at least, by her inherited gold claim.

L'Amour presents his 'good' women, his ladies, as a civilizing influence on their men, and by implication on the frontier itself. His heroines often restore their men to a domestic life they have lost through various unfortunate experiences. Ruble Noon, for example, has a strong sense of home as a higher ideal for a man, and is deeply attracted to the 'love and warmth of (the) quiet house' of the Mexican family who assist him. He had been 'Driven to desperation' but on seeing Fan Davidge, 'he knew how much he wanted to live. She trusted him… She had placed her faith in him, and he could not fail her.' Love for a good woman can make a man better, and braver. Ironically, Laurie Shannon's comfortable, feminine home and the stability she offers seems to put her out of Matt Coburn's reach – he recognizes that he has more in common with the less 'pure' Madge Healy, 'We've both been drifters,' he says. Madge echoes this, describing them as being 'homeless as a pair of tumbleweeds.'

L'Amour also demonstrates that women are often catalysts, helping fundamentally good men to succeed. His work is replete with examples of this phenomenon – Lilith Prescott and Cleve Van Valen, Ann Farley and Barney Pike are just two cases in point. But there is also a sense that this domestication, this 'taming' of men, cannot be achieved without some cost. Linus Rawlings deeply loves his wife Eve, but can't forgo his mountain wanderings.

The refining influence of women is not confined to home and hearth alone. Education is also one of L'Amour's recurring themes, and as in his own background, it is often women who introduce this concept to the male characters. After he meets Ann Farley, Barney Pike takes up a copy of the History of England, which he hadn't considered opening until he spoke to her. 'If a girl like that could learn something… by reading, I might learn something myself by studying. And if I was going to make something of myself, I'd better get down to brass tacks and do something about it.' Barney suddenly seems to discover ambition, realizing that he could achieve more than 'a day's work for a day's pay.' But educational aspirations can also seem incompatible with the rough and ready life of the West. Bess Chantry wants her son Tom to 'go to school back East. I want him to have a fine education.' This harking back to the East is often a reflection of weakness, either malevolent or benign, in his women characters. The appalling Peg Cullane misses the soft (implicitly corrupted) life of the East, while the innocent, but slightly feeble Juliana Ragan is Eastern in her thinking, and needs the protection of her tougher, Western-minded sister.

Mothers are highly valued, almost sanctified in L'Amour. Men who have been raised without a softening maternal influence, like Mike Bastien (in SON OF A WANTED MAN) may well go on to become good men, but their undiluted male upbringing can leave them vulnerable to bad influences. Mike realizes that his adoptive father has led him on a path that could divide him from the woman he loves, and put him beyond a decent life. 'Once he stepped over that boundary that separated the thieves from honest men it would not be the same.' At the other end of the moral spectrum, Charlie the dying outlaw calls on his mother in his hour of death – as though she were a saint – 'ma would find him. She always had, She's know what to do.' This pathetic cry seems to mark him out as fundamentally less depraved than his cohorts Janish and Lang who have led him into this desperate situation. The untimely death of matriarch Prescott seems to affect her youngest son very much for the worse. Zeke goes on to become a brutal outlaw and casual killer.

'She had placed her faith in him, and he could not fail her.' Love for a good woman can make a man better, and braver.

Remington Double Derringer

In SON OF A WANTED MAN, Drusillia Ragan is obliged to take responsibility for protecting her mother and sister, in the absence of her father. The ranch is isolated and we hear that there has been 'trouble in town,' 'We'd have to fend for ourselves' she says to her sister Juliana, 'that's why you should learn to shoot. Someday you may have to.' She takes a Derringer that her father has given her, checks that both barrels are loaded, and

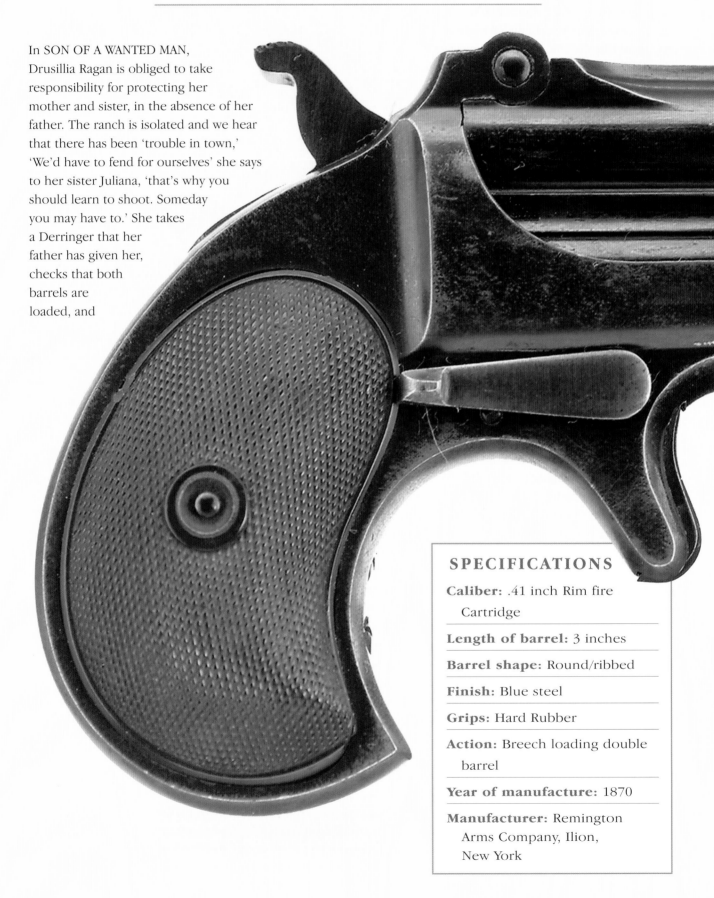

SPECIFICATIONS

Caliber: .41 inch Rim fire Cartridge

Length of barrel: 3 inches

Barrel shape: Round/ribbed

Finish: Blue steel

Grips: Hard Rubber

Action: Breech loading double barrel

Year of manufacture: 1870

Manufacturer: Remington Arms Company, Ilion, New York

Above: A neat piece of the gunsmith's art designed to fit into the daintiest purse.

synonymous with all weapons of the type. The press report on John Wilkes Booth assassination of Abraham Lincoln wrongly speled the name of the weapon used as a Derringer and this version of the name became common usage.

In the early days, many of these guns were single-shot weapons that relied on a well placed first (and only) shot to stave off an attack – the pressure was on to provide better odds. The two-barreled version that Drusilla carries, the Remington's Double Derringer, would have leveled the stakes considerably, particularly when an assailant was unlikely to expect that a respectable woman would be armed.

slips it into her skirt pocket. The Derringer was a popular choice as a defensive weapon for frontier women. It was easily concealed in a purse, the pocket of a crinoline dress, or even tucked in a ladies garter. It was named for Henry Deringer, a Philadelphia gunsmith who developed a range of compact, high caliber pocket pistols that, despite their size, had reasonable stopping power. His guns were so successful that his name became

Right: Even the fixing screw for the handgrip was delicately designed.

Louis L'Amour Filmography

It is now over fifty years since the release of the first film based on a Louis L'Amour story, HONDO. Not a bad start, with a cast headed up by John Wayne, and directed by John Farrow. From the early '50s, Louis L'Amour's work has been adapted into a major collection of Hollywood films and TV movies. This is hardly surprising – apart from the strong interest in their subject matter and the commercial success of his work, L'Amour's highly visual writing style naturally lends itself to the screen. Not only do his stories have great plots pushing them along with a vital narrative drive, but his characters, locations, and the fantastic sweep of the Western landscape itself are so vivid that they virtually jump from his pages. His writing style is very cinematic, and his scenes and dialogue can be lifted almost directly from the page. L'Amour's use of dramatic irony and coincidence also lend themselves to great cinematic moments.

The quality of the storylines and the complex characters obviously appealed to the cream of contemporary movie actors. John Wayne, Sophia Loren, Sean Connery, Brigitte Bardot, Yul Brynner, Richard Crenna, Leonard Nimoy, Natalie Wood, and Tom Selleck are just some of the glittering stars that grace productions based on L'Amour's work. The first rank of film directors, including John Ford and Sam Wanamaker, were also attracted to movies inspired by his novels.

Here is a listing of the major adaptations of his work, many of which are still available on VHS or DVD. The year of release is shown, and the source of the material is given in parentheses.

Hondo, 1953 (Story: 'The Gift of Cochise')
HONDO stars John Wayne as Hondo Lane, and is generally thought to be one of his seminal films. Geraldine Page is Angie Lowe, Ward Bond stars as Buffalo Baker, and James Arness as Lennie. The film was directed by John Farrow. The film runs for approximately 1 hour 41 minutes.

East of Sumatra, 1953 (Story)

Four Guns to the Border, 1954 (aka Shadow Valley) (Story)

Stranger on Horseback, 1955 (Story)

Treasure of Ruby Hills, 1955 (Story)

Blackjack Ketchum, Desperado, 1956 (novel, KILKENNY)

The Burning Hills, 1956 (Novel)
THE BURNING HILLS starred Tab Hunter and Natalie Wood as Trace Jordon and Maria Christina Colton, two of the most popular actors of the 1950s. Natalie Wood had starred in REBEL WITHOUT A CAUSE in the previous year, while Tab Hunter was most famous for his role in BATTLE CRY. Skip Homeier, Eduard Franz, Earl Holliman, and Claude Atkins also appeared in the movie, which was directed by Stuart Heisler. The film is in color, and runs for 1 hour 32 minutes.

Utah Blaine, 1957 (Novel)

The Tall Stranger, 1957 (aka THE RIFLE and WALK TALL) (Novel, SHOWDOWN TRAIL)

Apache Territory, 1958 (Novel, LAST STAND AT PAPAGO WELLS)

Guns of the Timberland, 1959 (Novel)

Heller In Pink Tights, 1960 (Novel, HELLER WITH A GUN)
HELLER IN PINK TIGHTS stars Sophia Loren (as Angela Rossini) and Anthony Quinn (as Tom Healy), as members of an itinerant theatrical troupe who perform in rowdy mining camps and cow towns. Interestingly, George Cukor, who was also responsible for MY FAIR LADY, directed this amusing romp, which also stars Margaret O'Brien and Steve Forrest. The movie was scripted by Dudley Nichols (BRINGING UP BABY) and Walter Bernstein. The film runs for approximately 1 hour 24 minutes.

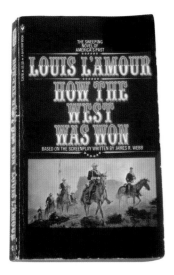

Above: HOW THE WEST WAS WON is a truly epic film based on an epic novel. Written in five strands, the Rivers, Plains, War, Iron Horse and Outlaws, all Western life is here.

How the West Was Won, 1962 (Novel)
HOW THE WEST WAS WON is a truly epic film, consisting of five interlocking stories brought to the screen by no less than three directors (Henry Hathaway, George Marshall, and John Ford). It contains some of the most legendary scenes in Western film history and has a fantastic cast of first rank actors including Henry Fonda (Jethro Stuart), Gregory Peck (Cleve Van Valen), Debbie Reynolds (Lilith Prescott), James Stewart (Linus Rawlings), George Peppard (Zeb Rawlings), Spencer Tracy (the voice of the narrator), and John Wayne (General William Tecumseh Sherman). The film was made by Warner Brothers, and runs for 2 hours 42 minutes.

Taggart, 1965 (Novel)

Kid Rodelo, 1965 (Novel)

Hondo and the Apaches, 1967 (Story, 'The Gift of the Cochise')
This feature was made up from material from the short-lived TV series, 'Hondo,' which was based on the original film, HONDO, starring John Wayne. Ralph Teager stars as Hondo Layne, Kathie Browne as Angie Dow, and Noah Beery Jr. as Buffalo Baker. The film runs for approximately 1 hour 13 minutes.

Shalako, 1968 (aka Man nennt mich Shalako, West Germany) (Novel).
The cast of SHALAKO is particularly glittering. Sean Connery stars as Shalako, Brigitte Bardot as Countess Irini Lazaar, and the cast also includes Jack Hawkings, Honor Blackman, Peter van Eyck, and Stephen Boyd. The film is in color, was directed by Edward Dmytryk, and runs for approximately 1 hour 53 minutes.

Catlow, 1971 (aka El Oro de nadie in Spain) (Novel).
CATLOW features Yul Brynner and Richard Crenna as friends Catlow and Ben Cowan in this amiable and lighthearted Western caper. Leonard Nimoy is the menacing Miller. This color film was directed by Sam Wanamaker, and runs for 1 hour 43 minutes.

The Man Called Noon, 1972 (aka Un Hombre llamado Noon in the Spanish version, and Lo chiamavano Mezzogiorno in Italy) (Novel)
This is a classic Western film, with fine performances from Richard Crenna and Stephen Boyd as Noon and Rimes respectively, and Rosanna Schiaffino as Fan Davidge. The film was directed by Peter Collinson and runs for 1 hour 27 minutes.

Cancel My Reservation, 1972 (Novel, THE BROKEN GUN)

The Sacketts, 1979 (Two novels)
'The Sacketts' is a made for TV mini series that charts the huge sweep of Louis L'Amour's Sackett family saga, concentrating on the Action of THE DAYBREAKERS and SACKETT. These novels seem to cover the entire gamut of the Western experience – cattle, gold, and violence in the untamed territory of New Mexico.

The massive cast of characters is drawn from the first rank of American actors, including Tom Selleck (Orrin Sackett), Sam Elliot (Tell Sackett), Jeff Osterhage (Tyrel

Sackett), Glenn Ford (Tom Sunday), Ben Johnson (Cap Roundtree), and Slim Pickens (Jack Bigelow). The action is directed by Robert Totten, and the series ran for a total of 3 hours 18 minutes.

The Shadow Riders, 1982 (Novel)
THE SHADOW RIDERS is an also made for TV movie, but its director, Andrew V. McLaglen, has a great pedigree in Westerns, having also directed SHENNANDOAH, THE WAY WEST, CHISUM and BANDOLERO. McLaglen also has a great cast to work with, including Tom Selleck (Mac Traven), Sam Elliott (Dal Traven), Ben Johnson (Uncle 'Black Jack' Traven), Geoffrey Lewis (Major Cooper Ashbury), and Jeff Osterhage (Jesse Traven).

Down the Long Hills, 1986 (Novel)
A made for TV movie.

The Cherokee Trail, 1986 (Novel)
A made for TV movie.

The Quick and the Dead, 1987 (Novel)
THE QUICK AND THE DEAD was a made for TV movie, directed by Robert Day. The feature had a solid cast, including Sam Elliott (Con Vallian), Tom Conti (Duncan McKaskel), and Kenny Morrison (Tom McKaskel). It ran for 1 hour 31 minutes.

Conagher, 1991 (Novel)
CONAGHER was a made for TV movie, directed by Reynaldo Villalobos. The cast includes Sam Elliott (Conn Conagher), Katharine Ross (Evie Teale), Barry Corbin (McCloud), and Billy Green Bush (Jacob Teale). Katharine Ross also starred in BUTCH CASSIDY AND THE SUNDANCE KID. The movie runs for 1 hour 56 minutes.

Shaughnessy, 1996 (Novel, THE IRON MARSHAL) A made for TV movie.

The Crossfire Trail, 2001 (Novel)

THE CROSSFIRE TRAIL was a made for TV movie, directed by Simon Wincer. It rejoices in the tag line 'A Hero is Measured by the Enemies He Makes.' The movie has a strong cast, including Tom Selleck (Rafe Covington), Mark Harmon (Bruce Barkow), Virginia Madsen (Ann Rodney), and Wilford Brimley (Joe Gill). It runs for 1 hour 35 minutes.

The Diamond of Jeru, 2001 (Short story)
THE DIAMOND OF JERU is a made for cable TV movie, written by Beau L'Amour. The cast includes Billy Zane (Mike Kardec), Keith Carradine (John Lacklan), Paris Jefferson (Helen Lacklan), Jackson Raine (Raj), and Piripi Warenti (Jeru). Unusually, the action of the film takes place in Borneo, but has all the usual action. The movie was directed by Ian Barry and Dick Lowry and runs for 1 hour 35 minutes.

Above: Louis L'Amour revived the legend of the American cowboy, and his novels continue to keep this Western icon alive.